In the book Breaking Solace, *the author skillfully guides the reader through Tali's journey to gradually realize her husband's true nature. She sees him for the narcissist he is and then begins to stand up for herself. The recap of some of the behaviors of a narcissist is a nice touch. I highly recommend it.*

Madison Frederick, Shifting Perspectives Coach,
Author of *Untangle The Web Of Narcissism from
Deceit and Chaos To Finding Your Sanity*

Tali navigates a toxic relationship with her controlling and manipulative husband, whose seamless shifts in behavior, combined with his confident yet sly style, keep Tali wondering what is real and what isn't. His power ego has Tali questioning her own sanity. How much does one endure in a narcissistic relationship? Can the narcissist ever change, or does the relationship have to change? Tali takes you by the hand down a rabbit hole to experience what a twisted narcissistic relationship is really like. Hold on...it's one hell of a ride.

Audra Harrold
Co-Founder and Executive Director of STL Fashion Alliance
Contributing Author in *Growth*, from the G.R.I.T. Series

This gripping novel offers a profound meditation on relationships with people suffering from narcissistic personality disorder. Through the tumultuous journey of Tali, a young woman in danger, plagued by the doubt of being responsible for the torments in her relationship, the author delivers a poignant and underlying message: it is essential to openly address difficulties in relationships, not to isolate oneself and to seek support when necessary. Breaking Solace, a book to read and share, to gain a better understanding of this real, delicate and complex theme.

Sophie Rouméas, Happy Author,
Transgenerational and Mindfulness Coach, Hypnosis Practitioner

Discover the enchanting world of Breaking Solace *and follow Tali's journey of self-discovery, courage, and friendship. This book is filled with emotions and life lessons that will leave you feeling inspired and grateful for the power of resilience.*

Maureen Ryan Blake, Founder
Maureen Ryan Blake Media

Emotions drive human interactions that shape our world. Skye Bellarmine leverages these emotions to draw you into Tali's emotional roller coaster. You can't help but root for Tali and follow her journey as she discovers her true strength.

Keri Williams,
Contributing Author to *Perfectly I'Mperfect,*
and *Survivor to Thriver*

BREAKING SOLACE

SKYE BELLARMINE

Star Skye Press LLC

Breaking Solace
Skye Bellarmine

Published by Star Skye Press, LLC, St Charles, MO / Dallas, TX

Project Management and Book Design: Davis Creative Publishing, LLC / DavisCreativePublishing.com
Cover Design: Missy Asikainen
Editor: Cheryl Roberts Oliver

Names: Bellarmine, Skye, author.
Title: Breaking solace / Skye Bellarmine.
Description: St. Charles, MO ; Dallas, TX : Star Skye Press LLC, [2024]
Identifiers: ISBN: 979-8-9888398-0-4 (paperback) | 979-8-9888398-2-8 (hardback) | 979-8-9888398-1-1 (ebook) | LCCN: 2023924060
Subjects: LCSH: Young women--Fiction. | Abused wives--Fiction. | Married people--Fiction. | Man-woman relationships--Fiction. | Codependency--Fiction. | Self-doubt--Fiction. | Narcissism--Fiction. | BISAC: FICTION / Women. | FAMILY & RELATIONSHIPS / Abuse / General. | FAMILY & RELATION-SHIPS / Abuse / Domestic Partner Abuse.
Classification: LCC: PS3602.E45733 B74 2024 | DDC: 813/.6--dc23

2024

Dedication:

To all diamonds in the rough…
it's your time to shine!

1

What Happened?

He left. The house is silent. Dazed, Tali touches her forehead and draws back a bloody hand. In horror, she reaches for the towel rack and collapses onto her knees, pulling the white bath towel down to the floor with her. She presses a corner of the towel onto her bloody temple to slow the bleeding. Total blackness ensues, her body responding to the attack with unconsciousness and shock.

The sun streams through the bedroom window as Tali awakens and tries to focus her eyes. Her head is pounding as she hears Blake's voice.

"Hey, sunshine!" he says. "How are you this morning?"

Tali begins to cry as she tries to speak. She reaches for her head to find a bandage on her left temple. "What's this? Why is there a bandage on my head? It hurts so badly."

"Just calm down, sweetheart. You don't remember last night, do you?"

"Why?" she asks. "What happened?"

"I'm not really sure. When we got home from dinner with Wren and Jess last night, you seemed disoriented. When I tried to help you up the stairs, you slipped and hit your head on the banister. I carried you up to the bathroom. The bleeding stopped fairly quickly when I applied pressure with a towel I grabbed off the rack in our bathroom. You passed out, so I bandaged your head and then carried you to bed."

Tali looks at him with doubt. She lays there quietly for a moment. Blake leans over to kiss her on the head, away from the bandaged temple, then suddenly jumps off the bed and leaves the room, whistling as he walks down the stairs. Tali stays unmoving in bed, still in pain, trying to remember the events of the previous evening. 'I should call Wren later this morning,' she thinks. 'She'll be honest with me about what really happened last night. At least, I hope she will.'

After Blake leaves for work, Tali calls her boss, Sydney Rowe, and tells her that she needs to work from home today. Sydney is concerned about Tali's labored speech as she senses Tali is in extreme pain. Is it physical or emotional this time? She can't tell. She okays Tali's request to communicate with clients from home today. Sydney hangs up when they finish the call. She's deeply concerned about Tali's well-being and safety. This isn't the first time Tali has requested to work from home this month. Something doesn't feel right.

"Beth," says Sydney, calling to her assistant, "please come in here."

"Okay. Be right there," Beth responds. She walks into Sydney's office and says, "What's up?"

Sydney turns from her drafting table to face Beth. "Tali just called to request working remotely today. She didn't sound good. I wonder what's going on with Blake this time. Remember two weeks ago, she requested a personal day. When she called that time, I could hear Blake yelling at her in the background."

"What exactly did she say when she called today?" Beth asks. "Any clues about what's going on?"

"Couldn't really tell," Sydney replies. "Her speech was labored, and she sounded like she was in pain and distracted. Let's you and I each call her at lunchtime today to check in on her."

"Sounds like a plan," Beth says with concern in her voice. "I hope she's okay."

"Me, too," says Sydney.

*****

The following morning, Tali strolls into Blanc, LeFitte, Landers, and Rowe Interior Design firm located in downtown Newport Beach to find her boss waiting in her office with her arms folded and a concerned look on her face. Tali walks into the office and closes the door behind her. She sits across from Sydney on the chaise and props her feet up on the ottoman.

Sydney takes one look at Tali and says, "What the hell happened to you?" Tali's eyes grow wide as she tries to answer the question.

"I don't exactly know," she says. "The blood…the bandage…the pain…the erased memory…Blake's sketchy story… I'm not sure what happened to me. Blake fed me some story about me falling and hitting my head on the banister when he was helping me climb the stairs after we got home from dinner with Wren and Jess two nights ago. I can't remember anything about the drive home or anything after that." Tali looks puzzled and in despair.

Sydney offers, "You should call Wren this morning and see if she can help fill in your memory gaps."

"Yeah, hope she can," Tali agrees as she looks out the window.

Sydney walks over to the chaise and puts her arm around Tali's shoulder. "We'll figure this out, dear. You're one of my best gems, and I'm going to do everything I can to help you come through this and shine."

Tali looks up at her with doubt in her eyes.

A few hours later, Tali finishes a conference call with a potential client. The call went well. She thinks she'll get the interior design job, which would be a half-million remodeling and redecorating project at a local law firm that's on the rise. Good visibility for her firm. She goes to Sydney's office to share the good news and then returns to her office, shuts the door, and settles onto the chaise to call Wren and get some answers after texting her earlier to schedule some time to chat. As she dials the number, her mind flashes back to Blake's explanation yesterday morning, which yielded more questions than answers.

Wren picks up, "Hello? This is Wren Jacobs."

"Wren…hi," Tali says hesitantly.

"Tali! Hi! How are you feeling?" Wren inquires, adding, "Blake called me and told me that you had a fall the other night after you got home. He said you might call me. What happened? You seemed fine when you two were leaving our place."

Tali replies, "I don't know. I woke up yesterday morning with a pounding headache, confusion, and a bandage on my head! Blake fed me some crazy story about me becoming disoriented as we were going upstairs and how he tried to help me. He said I fell and hit my head on the banister, and he bandaged my head and put me to bed."

"Wow," says Wren. "That's heavy. Is it true? What do you remember?"

"Nothing," says Tali. "I remember hugging you and Jess and saying good night as we left your house. Then, that's it. Waking up in pain the next morning is all I know."

"Okay, let's think through this, Tali. Something must have happened between the time you left our place and when you arrived at your home with Blake. Think, Tali. What do you remember?"

Tali closes her eyes and sinks down into her chaise lounge as she tries to recall what happened to her. Speaking aloud, she starts with hugging Wren good night and walking with Blake holding her left hand to the car. As he released her hand, he kissed her on the cheek and then opened her door and she got in. Next thing she recalls was pulling into their driveway. Blake opened her door and walked with her through the garage into the house where Jasper, their golden retriever, excitedly greeted them. She recalls Misty, the grey cat, stretched out on the floor in the hearth room. Then, her mind goes blank. "Wren, that's all I can remember."

Wren replies, "That's just bizarre, Tali."

"I know, right?" Tali says. "Guess I'll get back to work to try to get this situation off my mind for a while."

"Okay, my friend," Wren says consolingly. "I'll call you later. Take care. Love you."

"Love you, too," Tali says then sits there for a moment to collect her thoughts before getting up to go back to her desk. She closes her eyes and dozes off for about twenty minutes, dreaming of a scene where Blake is yelling at her and he hits her, causing her to fall and strike her head on the towel rack in the master bathroom. Then, he storms out of the room, and she sees herself trying to stop her head from bleeding by grabbing one of their white towels and then she faints. Tali awakens in a sweat and panic before realizing she'd fallen asleep in her office. She stays still for a few minutes.

Sydney glances through the interior window while passing Tali's office. Noticing the distressed look on Tali's face, she opens the door and rushes to her side. "Tali, are you okay? What happened?" Sydney gently inquires as she reaches for Tali's arm.

Tali replies, "I must have dozed off after I talked with Wren. OMG, Sydney, I just dreamt that Blake attacked me! In my dream, he hit me and I fell against the towel rack where I injured my head. I don't know if the dream is reality or fiction. Is my memory of two nights ago returning?"

Sydney sits down beside her and listens as Tali hypothesizes, unloading her angst and concerns and sharing the details of her dream.

*****

At home that evening, Tali is cooking dinner with Jasper standing by her side waiting for Tali to "accidentally" drop some morsels when she hears the garage door open and Blake appears in the doorway. Misty lays quietly in the nearby hearth room. Jasper greets Blake by jumping and wagging her tail. Blake bends down to wrestle with the dog as he says, "How are my ladies?" Jasper barks and Tali says, "Hi." Misty stays where she is and purrs quietly. Blake gives Tali a quick peck on the lips as he walks over to the desk to put down his keys and unload his pockets. He then goes to the fridge, opens the door, grabs a beer, twists off the cap, and picks out a koozie from the pantry. As he pushes the bottle into the koozie, he turns to Tali and says, "I think I had the worst day I've ever had…really bad…" and his voice trails off.

Tali asks, "Why is that? What happened?"

Blake sinks down into a chair and tells her the details of his day. "First," he says, "the check engine light came on in the Jeep on my way to work and the traffic was backed up on the interstate, so I had to start my first meeting on the phone while sitting in traffic staring at the engine light. Then, my boss, Adam, was sitting in my office when I arrived to meet the new guy, Joe, whom I hired two months ago. Adam says Joe has potential, but I'm not mentoring him well. Joe's complaining about me, saying I'm not communicating with him on the asset allocation project we are working on for the firm's new start-up client that I told you about last week. Nobody likes me there, Tali. I need to find another job. And I know you've been busy, so I didn't mention my latest performance review. Adam still says my staff are complaining that I don't listen to them and their ideas and that I'm not flexible. My team members are still telling Adam that I always have to have things my way and that I always have to have the last word." Blake stares at his beer as he spins the koozie around the bottle.

Tali continues stirring the veggies and then goes to check on the chicken roasting in the oven while she thinks about what to say this time. She has listened to Blake complain about his troubles at work ever since they started dating and now into their young marriage. He started this new position at the company six months ago. She begins by saying, "Blake, you've only been there for six months. Are you sure about what you heard them say? Maybe Adam is only trying to point out skills you need to work on so that you can be more successful. What do you think?"

Blake scowls and retorts, "You weren't there! Adam showed me the 360-degree performance evaluation results from my co-workers: above, lateral, and below. Tali, I think circles around most people in that company, and they had the nerve to rate me poorly." He looks at her with hurt in his eyes, yet also shadowed by a depth of darkness. She is silent.

"Let me think about this," she replies after she removes the chicken from the oven. "How about I make us some plates and we watch a movie while we have dinner?"

"Sounds good. I'll go look for a movie on the DVR," he replies as he shuffles into the family room.

'Whoa,' Tali thinks, 'here we go again. I'm so tired of hearing him complain about everyone at every job. I need to figure out a way to help him not be so irritating to people, at work and at home. Even my friends don't like him. Yesterday, when Sydney overheard him talking to me on the phone at work, she asked me why I let Blake treat me like shit. I should figure out a way to help him, but I'm already so tired all the time from him yelling at me and trying to control me that it's just easier to not say anything to him and leave him alone.'

Tali brings two dinners into the family room while Blake tries to find a movie that they both will enjoy. They settle on the new James Bond movie. They eat dinner in silence with occasional comments on the movie scenes.

When they finish eating, Blake moves over to snuggle next to Tali. He asks, "Would you like some port or some coffee?"

She replies, "How about an Irish coffee?"

"Sure thing. Coming right up," he says, as he pauses the movie before going to the kitchen. A few minutes later, he returns with two steaming Irish coffees and some gingersnaps. He knows how Tali loves gingersnaps with her coffee.

"Ooh, that looks nice! Thanks," says Tali as he hands her a coffee and then places the plate of cookies on the glass-top coffee table. Jasper was asleep under the coffee table, but now she is awake and sitting, tail wagging, waiting for a gingersnap. She, too, loves them. Tali breaks off a small piece of her cookie and says, "Speak!" to Jasper. Jasper responds with a low-pitched "rowl" and then lays down to say she's ready for her treat. Tali holds the cookie piece near Jasper's nose, and she gently takes it. Then she licks Tali's hand in gratitude.

Blake watches this exchange between his ladies with a little smile on his face. He thinks, 'Tali has a way with everyone, people and animals alike. Everybody loves her. I wish I had her charisma and ability to make friends so easily. She has moved fifteen times in her life, and she still has friends all over the country who love her. I just don't get it. I'm smarter than her.'

After the movie ends, Tali turns off the TV and collects the dinner plates to take them to the kitchen. She scrapes the plates and puts them and the silverware into the dishwasher. She stores the leftovers, finishes cleaning the kitchen, and extinguishes the candle she lit when she started cooking dinner. When she passes the sofa in the family room, she notices that Blake is still asleep after dozing off halfway through the movie. 'He's had a hard day,' she thinks as she covers him with a blanket without waking him and turns out the lights before climbing the stairs to the master bedroom. Jasper is already upstairs snuggled into her doggie bed next to Tali's side of the bed. Misty is relaxing at the end of the bed. Tali washes her face and changes into her sweats. She gives Jasper and Misty each a good night pat and turns on her laptop computer to work on the draft of her presentation that she's planning to discuss with Sydney tomorrow. It's for a conference she is speaking at next week. She has some new ideas that she needs to add to the file before she calls it a night.

2

Are You Awake?

Tali awakens at 5:30 a.m. She lies still and thinks about her schedule for the day. She has a kick-butt workout with her trainer, Ryan, during lunch today and meetings before and after. Gonna be a busy day. Then she hears, "Tali, are you awake?" She lies still before finally replying, "Yes, but I don't feel like talking."

He says, "Did you take my jacket to the dry cleaners yesterday and call the plumber about the guest bathroom sink? Oh, and could you call the names of the tire places I gave you to get three bids on tires for your car? You should get that scheduled this week. And I've been thinking about what Adam said to me in my performance review yesterday. I would like to talk with you about some ideas I have."

Tali sits up on the side of the bed to collect her thoughts, then gets up and walks out of the room.

"Where are you going? You're running away…again," Blake says.

She replies, "I'm not running away. It's 5:30 in the morning, and I'm going to get some coffee and sit in the hearth room for a little while and watch the sunrise while I think about my presentation for work. We can talk over dinner tonight."

Blake sighs heavily and exclaims, "Whatever," as she exits the room with Jasper following closely behind her. Misty has already moved to her favorite spot in front of the window in the hearth room.

By 7:00 a.m., Tali is making a cup of coffee to go when Blake comes up behind her and hugs her while kissing her passionately on the side of her neck. He whispers, "Let's make up tonight. How about dinner at that new beach restaurant on Main and we can talk?"

She says, "Okay. That would be nice. We need to make some changes and work this out."

"I agree," he says as he turns her around and kisses her on the mouth. Then he whips his left hand from behind his back containing a tissue and her lip liner and lipstick. "Brought these in case I messed up your lipstick with my surprise make-up kiss. How'd I do?"

Tali just smiles and blows him a kiss as she takes the lipstick, then grabs her coffee as the Keurig finishes filling her travel mug. She hugs him and they kiss goodbye with plans to meet for dinner.

On her way to work, Tali pulls off the road into a nearby park. She sits quietly for a moment and then opens her journal, a red book she has named Josie, like the cartoon redhead of Josie and the Pussycats. Tali writes:

Dear Josie… Today Blake woke me up at 5:30 a.m. again just to tell me what errands to do and what calls to make and to remind me of all the tasks that I hadn't completed from yesterday. I'm so tired of his judgment and criticism of me…every day. Last night he went on and on complaining about his job again… I just listened… I really don't know what to say anymore. I try to be supportive and empathetic. But I'm beginning to wonder if he's the catalyst for the troubles he's experiencing at work. Only time will tell. I'm trying to recall what excited me to get to know him in the first place. Thinking… I'm trying to put the puzzle pieces of my life together in my mind. I wonder if other people have relationship challenges like I'm experiencing with Blake right now… Where are his rages and harsh comments coming from? Things are different now. I did not see this coming.

Josie, thanks for not judging me. Thanks for being my safe place…much like my art room will one day become. I need to take more walks on the beach.

After stopping to write in her journal and then pondering the events of the past few days while driving to work, Tali arrives and greets the office manager, Allie, with a smile and a high five as she exits the elevator. Yes, she takes the elevator this morning. She's not in the mood. She marches briskly down the hall straight to Sydney's corner office and knocks while standing in the open doorway.

"Come in," Sydney says with her back to the door as she is sitting at her drafting table looking over some new design sketches. She turns to see Tali and says, "Hey, what's up?"

Tali asks, "Do you have a few minutes?"

"Sure," Sydney replies.

Tali closes the door and takes a seat in the director's chair beside the drawing table. "I'm not sure what's going on with Blake. He acts one way one minute and then rages about something the next minute and then he wants to kiss and make up, and then he gets mad, again, over seemingly nothing, and then he's buying me a gift or bringing me flowers later. He's just a living, breathing paradox! I don't know which way the wind will be blowing every time I'm around him. It's unsettling. I feel like I'm always walking on eggshells around him. And then, get this. My friend, Molly, called me yesterday. He called her to ask questions about me, and he told her that he thinks I'm having mental issues. I'm not sure who else he's spoken with or plans to speak with. Sydney, what should I do?"

Sydney starts with, "Okay, now let's think about this calmly. You are fine. You're not having mental issues. Sounds like Blake is the one who's losing it. You need to start keeping a log of his words and actions. Can you think back to when he started his bizarre behaviors?"

"Hmmm…let me think back. Probably about two weeks ago things seemed to get worse," Tali says.

"Okay then. Did something happen at his work about that time that you know of?" Sydney asks.

"I think a coworker got promoted. I talked him down because he's still new there. Then, more recently, he got his six-month job performance review, and everyone participating in the review said he needs improvement and listed the categories he needs to work on. He raged over that. He also raged at me when an old girlfriend of mine surprised me with an invitation to go on a girls' weekend with our college friend group next month. I have no explanation for why he's acting the way he does. It's as if anyone around him who is happy or gets good news, it makes him mad…or jealous, I guess? And he always says he's the smartest person in the room, at the company, etc., and each time the poor performance evaluations occur, he feels slighted and feels everyone is against him and doesn't like him. His current job was supposed to be a fresh start for him. We spent our own money on training courses for him to work better with others and learn how to better understand other people's personalities and working productivity styles. A lot of good that did. What a waste of money. Or would it be even worse if we hadn't invested in him?"

"Wow," Sydney says. "I definitely think you need to keep a private log of Blake's behaviors—daily, if necessary—in case you need evidence and documentation if or when you decide to get him some therapeutic help. In the meantime, Tali, I'm here for you. If you need a place to crash or you need some time to sort out everything, please let me know."

"Thanks. I think throwing myself into my work right now with the new design layouts is the best thing for me to do. I'm telling myself to focus. Definitely need a lunch workout today! Thanks for listening, boss," Tali proclaims as she opens the door and exits Sydney's office. She strides to her office with a new sense of confidence that she can handle whatever is going on with Blake and his mood swings. She's ready to start her day. First up is the meeting with the Newport Beach Convention Center event coordinator to brainstorm modifications for the space. Tali has a few minutes before she must head to the meeting. She writes…

Dear Josie... I talked with Sydney this morning about Blake's bizarre behaviors. She thinks something happened at Blake's work to trigger his rages at me. Could be...but that doesn't justify Blake's behaviors toward me lately. I wish I could convince him to go to marriage counseling with me, but he refuses. He says we're fine. But he's been contacting my friends and telling them that he thinks I'm having mental issues. I should confront him. I just don't want to make him mad at me.

3

When Monkeys Fly

Blake is in his cubicle meeting with Joe when his phone rings. He takes the call and walks down to the lobby and out of the office building to talk with Tali's college friend, Bentley. Tali and Bentley have always had an extremely close, platonic relationship. They tell each other everything. Bentley is working on Wall Street but plans to bring his security trading experience back home to California and launch a venture capitalist firm. He already has investors waiting in the wings for his start-up.

Blake says, "Thanks for calling me back, man."

"Sure thing. No problem. What's up?" Bentley inquires.

Blake says, "I'm worried about Tali. She fell a few nights ago. She's been acting a little strange lately. Can't quite put my finger on it. She says she feels fine, but my gut tells me something's going on with her. Has she said anything to you?"

Bentley says, "No. She called me yesterday and she seemed like herself—sharp and quick-witted. She's giving me grief over my new girlfriend, Tesca, the attorney from Italy who literally thinks circles around me and lets me know it. Tesca is an awesome lady, and I can't wait for those two to meet! Tali said maybe December would be good, or maybe New Year's. Tesca and I would love to get out of NYC for New Year's. I know that's the opposite of what most people say. It's different when you live here all year. I love NYC, but not the crowds on holidays."

"Sounds good. We would love to see you and your new flame during the holidays. So, you don't have any concerns about Tali's state of mind?"

"No. She sounded fine to me," Bentley replies. "Hey, I gotta go. Client meeting. Let's catch up again soon. Bye, Blake."

"Okay, thanks, Bentley. Sounds good. Catch ya later," Blake says, ending the call. He walks back into the office building and stops by Joe's cubicle after getting off the elevator. He says, "Joe, sorry about that. I had to take that call. So, let's get back to the asset project. I'm listening. What questions do you have?"

Ten minutes later, Bentley makes a call. "Tali, hey, can you talk for a minute?" As he talks into his cell phone while sitting at his desk in his sixteenth-floor office, he looks out the window at the rain pouring down on the city.

"Sure, I always have time to talk with you. What's up?" Tali inquires.

Bentley replies, "Blake called me to talk about you. He thinks something is going on with you, like mentally or something. He sounded strange, as if he were trying to gaslight you. It was weird."

"Oh my goodness, Bentley, he's been acting more odd than usual the past few days. Did he mention my supposed fall that I told you about yesterday?"

"Yes, he did," Bentley says. "He seemed concerned about you and wanted to know if I had noticed anything unexplainably strange about you lately. He was fishing, that's for sure, since he knows you and I are besties."

"Oh, Bentley, what is he trying to do? He's complaining about his new job, again, like he always does. He claims nobody likes him. They say he's inflexible and that he doesn't listen. And he just received a 'needs improvement' from his 360-degree performance review. I'm still concerned about the crazy story he told me about him trying to help me up the stairs and I fell and hit my head the other night. I had a dream yesterday about the incident — it sure played out differently in my dream. I don't know if it was a dream or maybe it's my recall returning. Molly recommends her therapist. She gave me her number. Think I'll call her. I need some answers."

"I agree, Tali," Bentley says. "You definitely need answers to solve this mystery."

"Thanks for calling to let me know about Blake reaching out to you. You're the best friend ever. Tell Tesca *buongiorno*!"

"Sure thing, girl. Catch ya later and stay well. Call me when you see the therapist. Ciao," Bentley says as he ends the call.

'I need to get some answers explaining Blake's strange behaviors and my recent memory gap,' Tali thinks. 'I pray that I do.' She calls her friend Molly to see if she's free for lunch tomorrow.

Tali arrives at the new beach restaurant on Main a few minutes early to meet Blake for dinner. Approaching the hostess stand, she tells the maître d' she's here for the Solace reservation for two. After looking at the reservation list, he picks up two menus and says, "Right this way, please."

Tali follows him to a table on the terrace overlooking the beach. The waves are rolling into shore, a few dolphins break the surface in the distance, and the sun is starting to set, creating an incredible backdrop for an encounter she is dreading. She's uneasy about being with Blake this evening. His recent behaviors are troubling her. She looks forward to scheduling an appointment with a therapist, hopefully this week, to try to comb out what appears to be the beginning of a difficult stage in their marital relationship.

The server brings two glasses of water to the table and inquires if Tali would like to order anything now. "No thank you," she responds. "I'll wait until my husband arrives. Thanks." Tali watches the seagulls and checks her email while she waits for Blake.

He arrives a few minutes later and leans in to kiss her before he takes his seat at the table. He smiles as he says, "Wow! You look beautiful! The sun setting behind you makes your blonde hair glow. Stunning." He smiles at her for a moment. She smiles in return.

"Thank you. It's been a long day. You know being near the water is always relaxing for me. I still see us building a beach house someday," she says, testing his reaction.

He replies, "We'll see about that. So, what's going on that made for such a 'long day' for you?"

"Well, hearing your list of directives and task list this morning at 5:30 was not the way I wanted to begin my day, then your yelling at me when I decided to leave the room and make some coffee was unnecessary. What's going on with you, Blake? Your criticism and rants are becoming more frequent and fatiguing and causing me to wonder about us," Tali says, looking to Blake for a reply.

He looks up at her, pauses, and then says, "Whoa, let's not start off the evening with accusations. You've been ignoring me more and more. You're at that gym with your personal trainer, Ryan, like every day. What exactly do you guys do during your 'workouts' anyway?"

"You noticed I've lost weight—twenty-five pounds since I started working out with Ryan. It was your idea that I join a gym and hire a personal trainer! I did, and you've enjoyed the results. You've been telling me how great I look. Is that a lie?"

"No, that's no lie. You look amazing. I'm sorry. How about I come to the gym with you sometime and you can introduce me to Ryan and show me some workouts?"

"Sure," she says. Blake reaches across the table to touch Tali's hand. At first, she starts to reject his advances, but then she reconsiders and allows him to hold her hand. He looks at her with those blue eyes that she fell in love with the first day she saw him. She wonders to herself, 'I can't believe next summer will be our third wedding anniversary. What have I done?'

He starts to speak and then retracts his hand and reaches into his coat pocket. He brings his hand back to hers, this time holding a small box that he presents to Tali. He says, "I know I haven't treated you right lately, and I know that I need to change. I hope this gift will help you to know that I love you, baby. I can change. I'm sorry. Can we work on this? On us?"

Tears well up in the corners of Tali's eyes as she opens the gift. The box contains the turquoise and silver bracelet that Tali saw last month when they vacationed in Mexico. The jewelry store had been closed when they went back to get the bracelet on the way to the airport. "Oh, my, Blake, you remembered how much I loved that bracelet. Thank you."

Blake removes the bracelet from the box and places it on Tali's left wrist. They hold hands and look into each other's eyes for a moment. The server comes by to see if they are ready to order. They agree and place their orders. Conversation during dinner includes plans for vacations and future adventures. Neither Tali nor Blake mention Blake's tantrums or his job difficulties or Tali's concerns about their relationship while enjoying a fresh seafood dinner and watching a breathtaking sunset over the Pacific.

"You know," Blake says with a smile, "our third wedding anniversary is coming up soon. Where would you like to go to celebrate?"

"You mean like a trip?" Tali inquires.

"Yes," Blake replies. "You mentioned wanting to do some driving trips in northern California. How about something like that? We could do like a five-day adventure…no rushing…stopping along the way to see the sights. I think it would be good for us to get away. What do you say?"

Tali smiles as she says, "That sounds wonderful!" They talk about sites to see while they enjoy coffee before leaving the restaurant.

While driving home, Blake says, "We should talk about our household budget sometime soon. I developed a new spreadsheet, and I've noticed some trends in spending where I think we can improve our cash flow each month. I'm trying to manage our cash flows so that we can reach some of those financial goals we used to talk about. I just have a few questions about expenses. I would be happy to walk you through my spreadsheet. When do you think we could sit down and chat for about an hour?"

Tali replies, "How about Saturday morning? The weather is supposed to be very nice. We can sit on the terrace and have coffee while we talk."

"Sounds great!"

Dear Josie: I'm not sure what's going on in Blake's head these days. Whatever "it" is, it's only getting worse. Tonight, he said that he was sorry for being mean to me and that he can change. And he gave me a bracelet to try to help solidify his apology. Gifts do not excuse him from treating me badly. But we did start making plans for our third anniversary trip. I'm looking forward to the away time with Blake. I love him so much. I still don't know exactly what happened to me that night. I need to talk with Molly and make an appointment with her therapist friend. I hope Molly can meet up for lunch this week.

4

Glad & Gloomy Switches

The next morning, Tali climbs the stairs to her office floor. Ryan convinced her that three flights of stairs each morning is a good way to start the workday. 'Not so sure about this in three-inch heels,' she thinks. She arrives at her office door and greets her coworkers with a bit of labored breathing and a smile. They laugh because they know her lunchtime workouts have been pushing her.

She walks into her office to see Sydney standing behind her desk, her back to the door while viewing the sunrise through Tali's plate-glass window. "I've been waiting for you," Sydney opens the conversation.

Tali replies, "Sorry. I didn't realize we had an early meeting scheduled for today."

"No worries, my dear. We didn't. I'm just inspired today to tell you the fabulous comments that your most recent new client called to share with me yesterday evening after you had already left."

"Sorry, I left yesterday at six to meet Blake for dinner," Tali says.

"Not a problem. I know. Your new client told me that you are 'Absolutely the most natural, artistically gifted and professionally trained interior designer she has ever worked with.' Tali, it's Cari who called me. She's the leading corporate community development consultant for fifty multinational corporations. She earns millions each year, and she thinks you are a gift from God to her firm. She looked over your designs for redecorating to create a new engaging office culture with fresh color schemes. And, if you crush the Newport office, she wants to send you to Paris to design their new office. What do you think?"

Tali is speechless. After the rough days with Blake's strange behaviors and questioning her reality, she didn't know how to respond to Sydney's relay of a client's unexpected reassurance and praise. "OMG, Sydney," Tali exclaims with tears in her eyes. "I totally didn't expect this."

Sydney faces Tali and smiles. "You earned this, girl. You're great, like I've always told you," Sydney assures her.

"You're the best mentor ever," Tali replies. Sydney smiles and then inquires, "How was your dinner with Blake last night?"

"Okay, but kind of guarded, if you know what I mean."

"Guarded in what way?" Sydney asks.

"I wanted to talk about his recent escalated mood swings and rants at me. He says I've been more distant lately, and then he said that he'll change and he gave me this bracelet." Tali holds up her left wrist.

"Wow, that's very pretty," Sydney says. "Like he thinks giving you a gift will make up for the way he's been treating you."

"I guess so," Tali replies. "But it won't. I'm scheduling an appointment with Molly's therapist friend to try to figure out what's going on. It's getting worse. I don't know what to call whatever behavior pattern this is... Or is it a pattern? He seems more and more chaotic in his comments and behaviors. I don't know..."

Sydney says, "You'll figure this out, Tali. Let me know how I can help."

Tali says, "You are helping just by listening and telling me that I'm not going crazy. Oh, and Blake wants to take me on a fun anniversary trip: five days driving up the coast to San Fran and Napa. Should be fun... I hope."

Sydney looks skeptical but approves the time off. She wants to help Tali. After Sydney leaves her office, Tali calls Molly to confirm their lunch plans. They agree to meet at noon at their favorite beachside café.

Tali confides her innermost concerns regarding Blake to her closest friend over a long lunch. "I feel like I've reached my limit in being able to tolerate Blake's chaotic, unpredictable outbursts. I often have rounds of uncontrollable tears while I'm getting ready for work, prior to appointments with my clients, and before going to bed. I frequently avoid taking Blake's calls during the day even if I'm technically available. My ringtone is even programmed to play the *Mission Impossible* theme song to alert me if the caller is Blake."

Molly responds, "Tali, we've known each other since junior high. You have changed. You aren't the fun-loving friend I have always known. You seem overly burdened. I've seen this creep over you since you married Blake. Do you think you need someone like a professional to talk to and figure out what's going on? I'm really worried about you."

Tali shares, "I really feel like I need a therapist to help me figure out what I'm dealing with. It's weird. Sometimes it feels like he has to mentally tear me down in order for him to get out of his depressed funk. I never know which version of Blake will be present when we're together. He rages at me over the most minor things, even in front of my friends. He may then offer to make me a cup of coffee using the kind voice he used when we were dating, or he'll bring home flowers the next day. It's just strange. I've been trying to get him to play golf with me since we started dating. I even had a custom set of clubs made for him two years ago for his birthday. He told me he would play golf with me, but he keeps making excuses. I finally gave up. I don't even mention golf to him anymore. Same with tennis. It looks like I'm gradually giving up my hobbies, but I have to go do his hobbies with him. If I have to go to one more poorly arranged trumpet quintet performance where he's tooting his horn… OMG…he makes me go to all of his concerts. Then he brags that he's always the best trumpet player there…ugh. It's taking a toll on my eating habits, my time to exercise, and my sleep patterns…even my time to paint." Tali sighs. Then she says, "He wants to take me on a third anniversary trip. We're planning to drive up to San Fran and Napa, like for five days. I'm hoping this trip will help us heal some stuff in our relationship. I love him, Molly."

Molly says, "I know you do. I think he loves you too. I know a therapist who helped me with my grieving after I lost my mom to cancer two years ago. I can call her for you if you'd like."

Tali, with a simple nod, wearily agrees.

Molly calls Tali back that afternoon and says her therapist, Dr. Shannon Cassidy, is booked solid for the next month. But Shannon graciously offered to have Tali come to her home on Wednesday night for an initial discussion of her situation. Tali asks Molly to let Shannon know that would be so kind and asks Molly if she would drive her there. Thinking ahead, she will tell Blake she is having a Girls' Night Out.

*****

On Wednesday, Tali meets Molly at a nearby restaurant for a quick early dinner, insisting it is her treat, then Molly drives Tali to Shannon's house, arriving at seven. Molly waits in her car in Shannon's driveway, pulling up a novel to read on her Kindle app.

Tali climbs the stairs to the front porch and timidly rings the doorbell. A woman, probably in her early fifties with a pleasant expression, answers the door. "Hi, I'm Shannon. You must be Tali."

"Yes," Tali says meekly, stepping inside. Shannon signals Tali to follow her into a study located off the family room. She closes the door and then motions Tali to sit down in a somewhat worn camel-colored leather recliner. Shannon pivots a side chair alongside Tali.

"Well, Tali, what brings you here?"

Tali softly replies, "First, thank you for letting me come to your home tonight instead of waiting for an appointment. My friend Molly speaks so highly of you."

Shannon notices the nervousness in Tali's voice and her hands gripping the chair arms. She says, "Tali, you're very welcome here. I asked my husband to go downstairs to the rec room to watch TV while we meet, and our two teenaged boys are upstairs working on their homework, I think." She smiles and grabs a legal pad and pen off the desk. "When Molly called me, I could tell from what she shared that you may very well be in a situation that needs prompt professional attention. I didn't want my tight schedule to put you at additional risk of emotional or any other form of what may be abuse. I have a few forms for you to fill out before we begin that will take about ten minutes. But first, I want to hear directly from you about your problem or chief complaint that brought you here."

As Shannon takes notes, Tali presents a snapshot of Blake's current behavior, essentially his impromptu rants over seemingly inconsequential events.

"Have you or Blake individually or as a couple sought out counseling?"

"I have begged Blake about every six months to seek counseling together or for him to seek counseling—whatever might work. He always responds that he doesn't need counseling in any form, as any perceived problem in our relationship is basically caused by me and only me."

Shannon next asks specific questions about Tali's background and family dynamics growing up, as well as what she knows about Blake's. Tali couldn't read her face as Shannon took notes, but her initial smile had faded, and two short perpendicular frown lines appeared above her nose.

Shannon speaks seriously, "Tali, thank you for all the information you've shared this evening. We need to wrap up and get you back home. I would like you to stop by my office and meet with my assistant tomorrow to finish completing the forms. You know that in any type of therapy, there's usually not just one visit. We could need weekly visits for a period of time and as much as a year with follow-up monthly visits. It depends on what a client is dealing with. I'm going to go back through my notes later, but before you leave tonight, I want to share with you a little technique you can use in most situations to deal with someone who upsets you. It helps you set boundaries so that the person is not allowed in your space spiritually, emotionally, or physically. It's called 'Glad & Gloomy Switches.' Imagine you are a stick figure and there are two square switches—like light switches—one on your chest and one above your belly button. Next, imagine the top one says 'GLAD' and the bottom one says 'GLOOMY' in all-cap letters. Now, imagine Blake being within arm's length of you where he can reach out and flip your GLAD switch and then reach out and flip your GLOOMY switch. He also controls the order in which he does this, which to you appears random such as GLAD…GLOOMY…GLAD…GLAD…GLOOMY…GLOOMY…GLOOMY…GLAD…GLOOMY…GLOOMY… Your one assignment is to go home and imagine that Blake cannot reach your switches. You control whether you are glad or gloomy going forward. Keep in mind, this is just a Band-Aid until we meet again. This in no way diagnoses or fixes anything related to the relationship that you and Blake have. I will tell my assistant to put you first in line if I have a cancellation with any other client, and I'll also ask her to start working you in on a regularly scheduled weekly basis in about a month. Let's stay in touch."

Tali says, "Yes, and thank you." Tears begin welling in her eyes, but they are hopeful tears.

Shannon shows Tali to the door. Tali numbly shuffles down the steps to Molly's car. On the way home, Tali and Molly stop at the beach parking lot for Tali to collect her thoughts. As she watches the waves roll into shore, she contemplates the session with Shannon. Then she thinks about Blake's bizarre behaviors. She and Molly talk while she loads her Amazon app and orders the book that Shannon recommended: *Stop Walking on Eggshells* by Paul T. Mason, MS and Randi Kreger.

When Tali gets home, Blake is asleep on the sofa with the TV on the show *24*. She turns off the TV and covers Blake with a blanket. She climbs the stairs to the upstairs room that will someday become her office/art room. She turns on a lamp and sits down to write in her red journal.

Dear Josie… The first session with Shannon was good this evening. I'm very thankful to Molly for recommending and reaching out to Shannon for me. She taught me about Glad & Gloomy switches. I'm ready to practice this technique when Blake starts in on me…like every day. I was sharing some background with Molly earlier today re: Blake's fake interest in my hobbies. I believed him when we were dating that we would do things together that we both enjoy. Guess he fooled me. Some people fake their interests when around other people to try to get the other people to like them.

Out of curiosity, Tali googles the name "Blake," finding the meaning "black/dark or bright/shining or pale" per the online dictionary. The name Blake is a mysterious paradox… 'Just like Blake himself,' she thinks before continuing in her journal:

Hopefully the awesome anniversary trip that Blake is planning for us will make a positive difference…help close the gap in some of our relationship issues.

5

Fear Sets In

The next morning, Tali gets up while Blake is still sleeping and goes downstairs to the kitchen. Jasper and Misty follow her. Misty climbs her cat tree in the family room and perches on top with her favorite toy bird. Tali makes coffee and takes Jasper for a walk. They arrive back home after about an hour.

Blake is sitting on the terrace with his coffee and staring at his iPhone. He says, "Hi! Where did you ladies go?"

"For a nice walk, since it's such a beautiful morning," Tali responds and asks Blake how he is doing?

"Doing great," he responds. "Just catching up on the news. What dinner plans do you have tonight? Another girls' night out like last night?" he asks wryly and then laughs shallowly.

"No plans tonight," Tali says. "Let's do dinner at home."

"Sure," Blake says.

After feeding Jasper and Misty and getting ready for work, Tali steps into her future office/art room to write in her journal for a few minutes.

Dear Josie… I am so afraid of Blake. His mood swings are so chaotic. I cannot figure out a pattern to his rages… What is the catalyst? He seems fine this morning. I still don't know what happened to me that night when my head was bleeding. I may never know. I don't think Blake's explanation fits the scenario. If only Jasper and Misty could talk…they were there that night.

She calls Bentley while driving to work to talk about the session with Shannon. Bentley answers the call. "Hey, Tali! What's up?"

"OMG, Bentley! Blake is yelling at me every day over basically nothing! And then this morning, he was unusually calm… but he's gonna rage at me tonight. I know he will."

Bentley says, "Okay… Okay, babe, let's just talk about this. I'm here for you."

She says, "The first session with the therapist was interesting. She taught me a technique to keep Blake from manipulating me at his whim. I'm still so confused."

Bentley asks, "What can I do to help you?"

Tali replies, "I don't know. Be there when I cry out for help?"

Bentley says, "Of course. Do I need to fly to California right now?"

Tali replies, "Not yet. Thanks, though. You're the best, dude."

"Okay, babe… I've got your back."

6

He Screams

Later that day, Tali and Blake turn onto their street at virtually the same time. Blake pulls into their garage first and Tali follows. They say their hellos as they exit their cars. It's seven o'clock, and both of them are very hungry.

Giving Tali a quick peck on the lips as they enter the house, Blake says, "Let's order Chinese for dinner. I'm starving!" Tali agrees as she bends down to play with Jasper. Blake kneels down to pet Misty.

While they are stretched out on the floor with the dog and the cat, Blake asks, "How was your day?"

"Good," replies Tali. "I received more unexpected yet very welcome news about the new project I'm working on."

"Oh, do tell," says Blake emphatically.

"Well," Tali begins, "remember those drawings I did for the Newport office of that community development person?"

"Yeah, I think so… The one with monochromatic teals—I know, big word—I listen to you!" Blake muses.

"Yes, that's the one," Tali says with a smile. "Sydney told me that the new client loves my designs and if I do well on the Newport job, then she wants me to design the decor for the firm's new office they are opening next year in Paris." Tali waits for Blake's reaction.

His face is blank at first before he musters a smile and says, "That's great. Sounds like your boss and clients really like you. Must be nice," he adds bitterly, getting off the floor to go unload his pockets and placing his jacket and tie on a chair. He then grabs a beer from the fridge. After getting a koozie from the pantry, he looks at his phone to retrieve the Chinese restaurant's number. "What do you want me to order?"

Tali, kind of surprised at Blake's nonreaction to her good news, says, "Broccoli chicken and some hot and sour soup."

"Okay," Blake says and calls the restaurant. He orders dinner and then goes upstairs to the master bedroom where he changes into jeans and a sweatshirt. He comes back downstairs to the family room and picks up his laptop. He sits down on the far end of the sofa where he usually sits. Before turning it on, he takes a swig of his beer and turns to Tali, who is sitting on the other end of the sofa with a nearby reading light on, scrolling through her email while she waits for dinner to be delivered. She then remembers to turn on the porch light and jumps up to do so. Jasper jumps up with her thinking they might be going somewhere. Tali smiles and then heads to the laundry room to fill Jasper's dinner and water bowls. "There you go, little pup, you get your dinner too!" Jasper eats voraciously as she wags her tail. Tali checks on Misty's food and water bowls and refills both.

Blake raises his voice to say, "Hey, are you coming back in here?"

"Yes, just a moment. I'm getting a LaCroix. You want one?"

"No thanks," he replies. "I already have a beer." Tali returns to the family room with her can of sparkling water. She sits down on the sofa.

Blake says, "Don't you think you should work here longer before you start gallivanting all over the world doing decorating jobs? I mean, you're still new at this profession. I wouldn't want you to get burned out too soon." He waits for her to respond.

She looks over at him and replies, "Apparently, I have a knack for developing fresh interior design ideas that bring to life the atmosphere the clients want for their spaces. Sydney is proud of me. She's my mentor. I've never had a real career mentor before."

"I know what you mean. I've always wanted a mentor. Seems like I only get bosses who have it out for me and promote everyone else around me even though I'm actually smarter than my boss and smarter than all those people around me," Blake says as he gets a little heated. "You need to help me, Tali. Maybe you could take some time away from what you are doing and help me figure out how I can be better at my job. I've always been supportive of you and your goals, babe." Blake's eyes grow dark as he becomes enraged. He suddenly jumps up and goes to the fridge for another beer. He comes back and sits down beside her.

Just then, the doorbell rings and Tali gets up to answer the door. 'Saved by the bell,' she thinks. She pays the delivery person, brings the food into the family room, and places the box on the coffee table. They open each dish in silence. She finally asks,

"Why are you so mad about me doing well at work? Aren't you happy for me?"

Blake takes a bite of his egg roll and then says, "I am happy for you. But I'm the man in this family, and I should be more successful."

"Oh, sweetheart," she says, "you're doing fine. You are very smart! You just have a few hiccups to overcome. You've only been working at the company for six months. You'll figure out the best way to manage people. You just need a little more time."

"Damn it, Tali! Don't talk down to me." Then he screams, "Stop being so condescending and patronizing me all the time! Just because everyone loves you and you are so creative, you're not better than me. I think circles around you, babe, every day!" He glares at her with eyes darker than black onyx. A sense of evil and uneasiness fills the room.

Tali puts down her chopsticks, gathers her dinner together, and takes it to the kitchen. She closes the boxes and stores them in the fridge. She fills her water bottle and climbs the stairs to the extra bedroom that will one day become her art studio. Her friends are coming over next weekend to help her start making her room design a reality by cleaning out the current storage in the room and bringing up her art supplies that have been stored in boxes in the basement since she and Blake moved into the townhouse last year. She opens the door and walks over to the corner table to turn on the lamp. She sits down on the papasan chair and holds her head in her hands for a few minutes to collect her thoughts. She flinches as she accidentally touches the scar on her left temple, triggering a memory she still couldn't really explain. She still cannot completely recall the sequence of that evening's events, especially her injury and Blake's supposed explanation. Tali closes her eyes as she tries to figure out what's going on in Blake's head.

She looks at her cell when the ringtone sounds. It's Bentley. She doesn't feel like talking and lets the call go to voicemail. Her phone dings when the voicemail hits. Then a text tone sounds and it's Bentley texting her. The message reads: "Hey - just have a feeling something's not right. Call me."

She sits there a few more minutes and then texts him back. "Wow! Your ESP is spot-on, my friend! Blake's on a rampage. I'm hiding in the spare room. Pray for me. I'll call you in the morning. Thanks for being you :)"

"Sure thing, Turt. Catch up in the morning :)"

Tali giggles a little as she thinks, 'Bentley always makes me smile when I need it. He hasn't called me Turt since college.' The nickname was short for Turtle. 'There's a story,' she thinks, recalling the memory with a smile.

7

Not Meant for Your Ears

After about an hour, she gets up from the papasan and turns off the light. She closes the door to the room as she exits so that Jasper and Misty will not go exploring in there. As she walks down the hallway, she hears Blake talking with someone in the master bedroom. The double doors are closed but slightly ajar. She stops just outside the doorway, out of Blake's line of vision. Through the crack in the door, she sees him sitting on the bed talking on his cell.

"Tali seems to be going through something. I'm not sure what it is. Her self-esteem seems low. That's probably why she's working out at the gym during her lunch hour. I told her that I'm going to go to the gym with her to meet her trainer and learn some workouts so that I can help her reach her goals faster. Jess, I am really concerned about her, man. Something's not right with Tali these days. Has Wren said anything?"

At that moment, Tali enters the master bedroom. Blake's eyes widen before he recovers with a smile. She says, "Tell Jess to give Wren my love, and I'll call her tomorrow."

"Okay," Blake says awkwardly. "I thought you were resting in the other room. Are you okay?"

"Yes, I'm fine," she says.

"Jess, I better go," Blake says. "Catch up tomorrow? Okay, sure. Sounds good. Good night." Blake puts the phone down and glances over at Tali. She says nothing and goes to the master bathroom to put on her sweats and get ready for bed. She grabs a book off her nightstand before pulling back the covers and snuggling into bed. She reaches to turn on the lamp and opens her book. Blake says good night, switches off his lamp, and turns his back toward her. She pretends to read, but she's actually thinking about the conversation she just overheard. What is Blake trying to do by telling their friends that he thinks she is not mentally well? Why is he gaslighting her? What does he see as the benefit of telling lies about her to their friends? Her schedule is stacked tomorrow, but she must carve out some time to talk with Wren and Jess about what Blake is trying to do behind her back. Tali texts Wren and schedules some time to chat tomorrow. Setting aside her book, she opens her journal and writes.

Dear Josie… I'm confused about Blake's behaviors. I have so many questions and no answers. I can't wait for my next session with Shannon.

Then she turns off the light and snuggles under the covers as she silently prays about everything going on, her thoughts reeling with questions.

8

Words Hurt… Let's Talk

The next day at 4:30 a.m., Blake wakes up and rolls over to put his arm around Tali. She doesn't move. Of course, she is now awake and wondering why he thinks putting his arm around her is the right thing to do after what he did to her last night. His rage during dinner and his defaming comments about her while talking with Jess were unconscionable. She's still angry. He needs to apologize, but as usual, he will not be sincere. She dozes off, and her 6:00 alarm comes a little too soon. She hits the snooze.

When the snooze alarm sounds, Blake is in bed staring at the screen on his smartphone. Tali sits on the side of the bed and contemplates her day. She stands up after a minute to go make coffee in the kitchen.

Blake gets up while Tali's in the kitchen and she hears the shower. They get ready for work in silence. When Tali is filling her travel mug with coffee at 7:30, Blake says, "I'm sorry about last night."

She replies, "We need to talk. We'll cook here tonight and talk about whatever this thing is that's going on with us. Does that work for you?"

"Yes," he says. "I can be home by seven."

"That works," she says. She pats Jasper and Misty before she leaves the townhouse through the garage.

9

Is He Yelling at You?

Upon arriving at her office, Tali works on the Newport Beach Convention Center design project all morning and then goes to the gym during lunch to train with Ryan. While they work out, she talks with him about trying to overcome people's hateful personalities and how to follow through on her goals: fitness, work, spiritual, personal. Blake has been lying and co-ercing Tali's friends to believe his lies about her. She confides in Ryan. Ryan listens attentively, knowing that personal trainers often also play the role of therapist…someone to encourage others through life's difficult circumstances.

Meanwhile at Blake's workplace, he is yelling at an employee in a meeting. "I told you how to calculate the returns!" Blake screams at Donna, who has been working at the company for only four weeks. Donna replies, "Okay, but you specifically instructed me to use the modified durations table values that you posted on the portal last week. Now you're telling me that I should have used a different table. Here are my notes with your instructions."

"Oh my God," Blake exclaims. "Do I have to do everything myself? Give me your spreadsheet. I'll finish the calculations. Just go away!" Donna quietly exits the conference room.

Blake sighs and stares at his computer. He doesn't realize that the whole staff heard him raging at Donna. Donna walks back to her desk…shaking. Blake's boss comes to the doorway of her cube and asks, "Donna, are you okay?"

"Yes, Adam," she replies.

"Was Blake yelling at you in the conference room?" he inquires.

"Yes," she says. Adam asks her to write and email that experience to him. He's keeping a log of Blake's interactions with coworkers.

10

Are You Okay?

At seven on the dot, Blake comes into the kitchen where Tali is chopping carrots for a salad. She has fresh broccoli with salt and pepper, drizzled with olive oil, roasting in the oven. A lit candle flickers as the ocean breeze wafts through the kitchen from the open terrace windows. Jim Brickman's "Escape" playlist softly plays in the background. Blake pats Jasper on the head and comes over to hug and kiss Tali. She doesn't feel like it, but she decides to accept his gentle kiss and embrace.

"How was your day?" Tali asks.

Blake replies, "Been better. Been worse. Yours?"

Tali says, "Pretty good. Finished the first draft of a design I've spent weeks on. Lunchtime workout was hard. I'm pretty sore." Blake empties his pockets onto the kitchen desk. He then shuffles over to the fridge to get a beer and twists off the top. He takes a long swig of the beer as he walks over to the pantry to grab a koozie. He approaches Tali and reaches to lift her chin to make her look him in the eyes.

He says, "Tali, I'm not sure what's going on with you… what's in your head these days. I just want you to know that I'm here to help you. You seem to be a little off. I'm concerned about you. Ever since your fall that night…" His voice trails off as he observes her. Then he adds, "Are you doing okay?"

Tali stares at him in disbelief. She's thinking, 'He's been gaslighting me, and now he has the gall to say that he cares about me? I don't even know how to respond.' She peers down at the salmon gently sautéing on the stove as she composes her response. "Blake, seriously?" she says, returning her gaze to him. "Your yelling and outbursts are getting old. And I didn't fall that night. I know what happened. I remember…" She watches for his reaction.

Blake's eyes begin to darken, and the color leaves his face. "You do?" he asks.

Tali stays silent before finally replying, "I don't feel like talking about it right now, but I would like to discuss your comments about me to Jess last night. My self-esteem is not low. Why did you lie about me?"

Blake looks down at his pale ale while thinking of a reply. He says, "Babe, I'm worried about you and all the pressure Sydney is putting on you at work. It has to be so hard working for her."

She says, "Actually, I love my job, Blake! Sydney's the best boss. She helps me. She doesn't hurt me. Blake, actually, you're the one who hurts me." Blake squirms a bit. She thinks he's waiting for her to bring up *that night*. Instead, she adds, "With your words."

His face displays relief. He tells himself 'She doesn't remember exactly what happened that night.' Out loud, he says, "I'm sorry. I can change. I know I always say, 'I am what I am,' but I really can change. I'll stop yelling at you."

"Really?" Tali asks.

"Yes," he says, placing his beer on the counter and fully embracing her. They stand there for a moment until the oven timer goes off. "Broccoli is done," she says. She picks up the oven mitts, turns off the oven, and removes the steaming pan of broccoli from the oven. "Let's sit on the terrace for dinner tonight."

"Sounds good." He goes outside to turn on the gas-burning lights since the sun has set, leaving the sky aglow. Tali sets the outdoor table while Blake serves his plate. The conversation during dinner covers some unchartered ground. They talk about their expectations of their marriage and ideas each has been pondering about what their future holds. Soon, the conversation stalls as they each turn inward. Tali contemplates Blake's earlier apology and his comments about trying to curb his yelling. She wonders how that's gonna go this time around… He's said those same words in the past and nothing changed. Meanwhile, across the table, Blake glances at Tali periodically and smiles a little as he ponders on how much she really recalls about "that" night…and how he said he's going to change, but he doesn't really see how he's done anything wrong. Tali's always the reason for the bad feelings and harsh moments in their relationship… She always has been.

11

Door #1...or Rather, Spreadsheet #1

On Saturday morning, Blake and Tali are sitting on the terrace having coffee. Blake has his laptop open to his latest budget spreadsheet and begins to walk Tali through the calculations. She notices a trend in outflows of their funds with a reference in the cell to another sheet. She has her iPad and is taking notes while Blake speaks. She asks a few questions and answers Blake's questions about her expenses to his satisfaction. He stresses that if they want to purchase a larger house next year, as they had discussed, and keep the townhouse and lease it out to tenants, then they need to start pinching a few more pennies. He asks her if she really still needs her gym membership. Tali assures him that she does. As his voice level escalates, Tali dilutes his impending rage by agreeing to bring her lunch to work more often and cook more dinners at home. He appears to calm down a little, but he is still glaring at his spreadsheet while she talks. After their conversation, Tali takes Jasper for a walk to the beach.

She calls Molly to talk while she and Jasper stroll along the shore. She listens as Molly shares some insights that she hadn't considered. She's hopeful she can talk with Shannon later this week if there's a cancellation in the therapist's schedule.

12

Counting My Blessings

On Sunday morning at 8:15, Blake sits quietly in his La-Z-Boy rocker recliner dressed in a polo shirt and khakis. He's ready to leave to meet Wren and Jess in thirty minutes for brunch at the country club. His personal laptop is balanced in his lap. He opens a folder containing several worksheets he updates every weekend based on closing stock market values as of the latest Friday. Stock prices were up Friday on a net basis, with the outlook predicting even stronger moves.

Blake looks over one worksheet indicating overall returns for each of his investments, including ten-year, five-year, one-year, year-to-date, and month-to-date as applicable.

He smirks as he closes the folder and shuts down his laptop, commenting, "Counting my blessings." He then calls out to Tali that it's time to drive to Wren and Jess's club for brunch.

During brunch, Blake shares the itinerary and plans he's making for his and Tali's driving trip to northern California.

He's going to surprise Tali by renting a convertible, but he's not telling anyone about that or the gift he's already purchased. He can't wait for her to see it when they arrive at the bed and breakfast in Napa, which will be on the day of their anniversary. Everyone around the table is impressed by Blake's travel plans. Tali says, "I'm so excited for our trip!"

13

Frog in the Pot

The following day, Monday, Tali stops by therapist Dr. Shannon Cassidy's office. She completes the necessary paperwork to be an official client, including medical history, HIPPA, and other forms. While there, she asks Shannon's assistant, Amy, if there were any cancellations yet that Tali could be substituted as a replacement. Amy checks and says, "We received a cancellation earlier today for this Thursday at 2 p.m. for a standard one-hour appointment."

Tali instantly replies, "I'll take it." She doesn't care what her own work calendar has booked. She would work around it.

Tali shows up early for her therapy session on Thursday with Shannon. As she enters the waiting room, she spots a seat in a corner, hoping no one she knows would coincidentally see her waiting for her appointment. Earlier that morning, she had quickly googled Shannon's credentials, noting that she was licensed in family counseling, so her therapy practice was focused primarily on family dynamics. Her undergraduate schooling in psychology was at the University of Oklahoma, while her master's and doctorate were from the University of Texas in Austin.

Shannon comes out into the waiting room and, spotting Tali, says, "Hi, come on back." Tali follows her down the hall and into her compact office. She motions to Tali to take a seat in a mid-century-style recliner. Shannon picks up a file folder off her desk along with a legal pad and pen. She pulls up a chair, sits down, and begins the conversation, "Tali, it is really good to see you here today. What kind of week have you had? Give me an update on where we left off when we talked at my home a little over a week ago."

Tali recaps life with Blake the last few days, specifically calling out his rage scenes. She mentions the anniversary trip that Blake is planning for them. She tells Shannon that she has been journaling about Blake's rages and the lies he has been telling others about her. "I have so many questions."

Shannon muses, "I see, and did you try keeping your Glad/Gloomy Switches at a safe distance during interactions with Blake?"

Tali responds, "I sort of tried, but it wouldn't occur to me automatically. I think I could use some help."

Shannon tells Tali that she's made a note to follow up doing role-playing with the tool. Shannon then says, "Tali, I've had you and your situation with Blake on my mind a lot since meeting you. Here's what I'm thinking: Today I want to get an idea of what is inside of your mind, heart, and soul with respect to your relationship and interactions with Blake. Next week I'll have you do a more formal assessment of how you perceive Blake's actions and reactions to life since it doesn't appear he will submit to counseling directly."

Tali nods. "Whatever you think is best."

Shannon thinks quickly and quietly to herself that she needs to get a read on Tali's self-worth by asking her several poignant questions. She notes on her legal pad that Tali looks like any typical woman in her early twenties. She is bright and would be considered relatively attractive with a kind manner with people. While there are no obvious outward clues of the wear and tear she is enduring, Shannon knows only too well that this is probably a deceiving facade. She could sense that Tali is feeling burdened…but by what exactly? And that, underneath the shell, Tali's psyche is gradually becoming more traumatized. She is reminded of the story that if you boil a pot of water and throw in a live frog, the frog will hop right out, saving his life to croak another day. If, on the other hand, you place a frog in a pot of cold water and turn the heat up slowly, that frog will stay in the pot. The frog will not jump out but slowly get used to the increasingly hot water until it boils the frog to death. Shannon prays that the hot water Tali is in has not gotten too hot for her. She adds to her notes that she isn't sure at this stage if there is any physical abuse involved.

"Tali, I've got some yes or no questions I am going to verbally run through with you."

Tali nods.

Shannon asks, "Are you struggling to tolerate Blake's strange and abusive behavior?"

Tali replies, "Yes. That is what brought me to see you. I cannot manage whatever this is by myself anymore."

"Next, are you walking on eggshells around him, always on alert?"

"Absolutely," Tali replies.

"Number three: Are you stuck in a revolving door, and when things are rough, you just keep going back, hoping it will be better this time?"

"Definitely. When things are calm, I hope it remains that way, but it never does. Many days there are only a few hours of calm; occasionally, maybe two days. Sometimes I get the silent treatment for several days. What's that quote about the definition of insanity as doing the same thing over and over again and expecting a different outcome? Am I going insane trying to ride this out, trying to figure out his behavior patterns? There is no pattern…"

"Tali, you're not going insane. We're figuring this situation out together. I'm here to help you. Okay, fourth, do you have conflicting feelings about Blake, such as 'I love him but at the same time I hate him'; 'He is both good and bad'; 'I trust him and I really don't trust him"?

"Exactly. I love him, but I'm also afraid of him."

"Do you feel you try to explain your situation to friends and family, but they don't understand?"

"I really don't try to explain this to anyone except to my mom and my closest friend."

"Finally," Shannon asks, "do you feel alone, exhausted, and confused due to this difficult relationship?"

"I really do. I pass out every night in bed after Blake judges or chastises me for something or other. I just hope and pray that he falls asleep each evening before I do so that I don't have to listen to his hurtful words. Also, he makes me have sex with him every night I'm still awake when he's ready to go to bed. I thought this was normal for married life until I started talking with some of my friends about it. They've been asking me why I seem unhappy these days and noticed my bright personality seems to be dampened more and more. Shannon, I feel like I'm becoming depressed. I need your help in figuring out how to keep Blake's rages from bringing me down. How can I help him deal with his emotions and feel better when I am so sad?"

"Okay, now, let's build on what you just shared. I have some additional questions that will dig a bit deeper, getting to how you feel physically, mentally, emotionally, spiritually. I'm going to ask about any intense emotions. Let's start with your body. Do you have any pains in your body?"

Tali replies, "None, except after my workouts with my trainer. Those are good pains though. Blake wants me to cancel my gym membership. I need the workouts, and he's the one who convinced me to get the membership in the first place."

"Do you ever feel panic, terror, or dread attacks, anxiety, stress, or depression?"

"Yes. All of the above when Blake enters the room. I never know how he's going to behave or what he's going to say."

"Do you feel unsafe, jumpy, vulnerable, don't know what to do next?"

"I do when Blake's around."

"Any obsessions seeking answers, playing 24/7 detective, or stalking the abuser (online or in person)?"

"No." Tali says. "I'm just trying to figure out why he's acting this way. It's getting worse…the yelling and rages…the lies he's telling others."

"Do you suffer from brain fog, insomnia, nightmares, waking up in a panic?"

"Sometimes."

"How about helplessness, hopelessness, powerlessness?" Shannon adds, "The dark triad is a real thing caused by abuse."

Tali replies, "I've been researching the dark triad. I read the original article… Wow… Blake's rating would be interesting to know."

"Are you doing ok?" Shannon asks. "There are a few more questions."

Tali nods yes.

"Are you feeling heavy shame, confusion, like 'How did this happen? Maybe it's my fault? Is it really abuse?'"

"Yes. I'm trying to look back through our relationship…the beginning. He was so sweet to me — like amazingly sweet — then things started to change after college…especially when we got engaged." Then, wanting so badly to still believe in their relationship, Tali adds, "Yet, I still love him."

"Are you feeling a loss of self, no control in life, not able to be who you really are?'

"My friends have been telling me that I'm not the same person I was before Blake entered my life. They say that I'm not as happy as I used to be before him. I want to be happy again… happy with him…like we used to be."

Shannon asks Tali to give her an overview of her history with Blake.

Tali doesn't hesitate, hoping that by telling Shannon, it will make more sense as to why she's stayed with him. "I met Blake at UCSD at the beginning of our junior year of college. I was an interior design major and Blake was a finance major. We met in our Suffragettes to Civil Rights writing class. Blake later admitted that he chose this course because he expected to meet girls in a women-themed writing class. Well, he was successful. He met me. On day two of the class, he asked me out, but I had other plans with my closest high school friends I grew up with who also attended UCSD. On day four of class, he asked me out again. I had other plans. Bentley, my best friend, and I were planning to hang out at the beach and have dinner with my parents that weekend. The following Monday morning while I'm on my way to class, Blake approaches me in the hallway and asks me out a third time. I agree to go this time. Our date was fun. We played tennis. I'm actually a tennis player. He wasn't, but he tried to impress me. He was cute. As the days and weeks followed, we played more tennis and went on walks around campus in the evenings. We attended some lectures on campus, and he took me to an incredible exhibit at the art museum. We spent quite a bit of time at the beach…cheap date for a couple of college students, right?

"I grew up in Point Loma, and Blake grew up on Mission Viejo. Our families both still live in those cities. I miss my family and occasionally visit.

"During my junior year of college, one of my professors, Dr. Eileen Gray, took a real interest in helping me get a summer internship. She's amazing! The internship was in Newport Beach with the firm where I currently work. God was definitely looking out for me when I crossed paths with Dr. Gray. Blake got jealous and tried to talk me out of going, but I went to Newport Beach and worked the entire summer after my junior year. Then Sydney, my boss, offered me a job after graduation! My family and friends were so excited for me. Blake was not." Tali paused then said, "I don't know why I couldn't see the red flags of his nasty, hateful controlling behaviors back then. Guess I was still in love with those blue eyes, which now turn black when he rages at me.

"The relationship journey continued during our senior year of college. Blake began applying for finance jobs. After a few months of interviews, a growth fund investment firm in Newport Beach offered him a job. He told me that he decided to accept their offer since I would be in Newport Beach. My parents and Blake's parents came to UCSD for the graduation ceremony. They helped us pack up both of our apartments in preparation for our individual moves to Newport Beach. At that point, I had a month before I started my new job. Blake had two weeks, and after we got there, Blake demanded that I help him unpack his new apartment first since I had more time before my new job started. I helped him for a few days and then I went back to my apartment when three of my best friends from high school arrived to visit and help me decorate my new apartment.

"Blake continued to call and text me many times each day to ask what I was doing while my friends were visiting. My friends kept wondering and asking me what I saw in this guy. I always brushed off their questions and said, 'I love him.' I totally enjoyed the week with my friends! We had fun going to the beach in between unpacking and decorating the apartment. After they left, I called Blake at work. He was cool and a bit short while we were talking. We made plans to meet at his place for dinner. I told him that I would pick up some groceries. We each had a key to each other's apartments. I said that I would meet him at his place that evening. He warmed up to that idea.

"When there was a week and a half before I was to start my new job, Blake wanted me to stay at his place and clean up his messes while he was at work. I helped him clean while he was there in the evenings that week, but I lived in my own apartment. I couldn't bring myself to be in his clutches 24/7. Why did I even agree to spend my free evenings cleaning up his messes and unpacking his boxes? I should have been hanging out at my place getting to know my neighbors and walking around the city more. What was I thinking? Why was it so easy to allow myself to fall into his web of control?

"Our families got more involved, with Blake's parents arriving one week before my job started and three weeks since Blake started his new job. Blake's mom has emotionally traumatized Blake his entire life—doubting him, telling him he's never good enough—which lowers Blake's self-esteem. She is very controlling, always directing everyone in how they should do a task—laundry, dishes, what to order at a restaurant, how to act at work, which sites to see. She always controls the conversation. Blake's father is quite mousy while in her presence. When I invited his father to run to the grocery store with me, his father talked a lot and was actually quite intelligent and funny. I began noticing that Blake doesn't treat his father with respect and often discounts or tries to correct what he says whether he's expressing an opinion or recalling details while sharing a story about a family outing. I asked Blake why he, his mother, and Blake's older brother, Thomas, pretty much ignored his father. He told me that his father had a mental breakdown years ago, and he still has emotional problems and to not pay any attention to him. I felt sorry for Blake's father. I really enjoyed talking with him when we went to the grocery store. Then Blake's parents returned home. My parents took us out to dinner that evening and then they returned home the following day. During the rest of that week, I spent most of my time prepping for my new job, exploring Newport Beach, learning my way around town, and thinking about life while going for long walks on the beach. Bentley called me a few times while he was prepping for his new career on Wall Street. It was a productive week—at least, I thought so. Blake went off on me a few times in anger. I just let him chill. We had a few good evenings that week. I cooked dinner for him the Saturday before I started work, then listened to him complain about his new job and how nobody at work liked him. I should have seen the pattern earlier. I don't know, Shannon. Now that I'm talking about this, I don't understand how I could have missed Blake's bizarre behaviors. They were there from the beginning, and yet I allowed him to charm and then manipulate me."

Shannon commented, "Charm can be very convincing, especially if you are truly in love."

"At Christmas that year, Blake proposed marriage to me. I gave it a lot of thought, and I talked with my parents. Thinking back about this time in our relationship, I now see how Blake was gradually increasing his control of me and my life. He was beginning to act like I was actually his property and was controlling our joint decision-making process more and more. He was scheming on how he could persuade me that I was a bad negotiator and how all our marital assets needed to be in his name when we get married. I fell for his lies hook, line and sinker. I let him manipulate me and convince me that he needed to be in charge of the finances. What was I thinking?"

"You weren't in a thinking place at that time, Tali. You were feeling a lot of things, especially with your new job. You were just getting started with your life."

"Then the wedding planning started, which was an interesting process. I quickly learned that Blake doesn't have any true friends. He convinced me that I should not have many bridesmaids so that the number of wedding party members on each side of the altar would be even. I had to leave some of my best childhood friends out of the wedding because Blake didn't have enough friends to be groomsmen. I should have stood my ground and built my bridesmaid tribe the way I wanted to. Again, what was I thinking? I can hear myself now, and what I'm hearing is that Blake made me unhappy from the very beginning. But that's where it gets especially ugly. I didn't realize it because he always made me think that I was too emotional and sensitive to his comments and rages."

Shannon said, "Thus began the traumatic life of being married to a narcissist."

Tali laughed, but it was a sad laugh. "It didn't take long after we were married for the honeymoon phase to morph into daily dramas and Blake's rages. He didn't like his job and ranted about how much he hated it, how all of his coworkers hated him. I would either stand in the doorway of the master bedroom each evening while he changed out of his work clothes and vented or listen while I was cooking dinner. It became rather tedious listening to his complaints day in and day out. Feels like his diatribes are going to continue into perpetuity… OMG."

"Does talking about this feel cathartic?" Shannon asked. "Can you see more clearly the behavioral red flags that a narcissist can bring into a relationship without the partner recognizing what they're doing, both behind their backs and right in front of their faces?"

"Shannon, I feel defeated. I've learned the art of talking without saying anything. I still communicate with Blake but with more of a grey-rock style of communication. I don't give him the material he might use with my friends and family to harm me."

"Those are known as 'flying monkeys' — the people that your partner tries to convince that you are falling apart, losing your mind. It sounds to me like your friends and family see right through him."

"They do. Why didn't I?"

"Have you heard of irrational loyalty to an abuser due to cognitive dissonance, like returning to an abuser over and over?"

"I still love him and want to help him work through whatever is going on with him. I just don't know what to do. I can't continue like this."

"That's why you're here. One last question. Are any addictions, like alcohol, drugs, shopping, getting worse?"

"I've been researching coping mechanisms," Tali states, deflecting the question. "I might be trying to channel my anxiety into my work. I need to start painting again. I think that might help."

On her way back to the office after talking with Shannon, Tali pulls her car into the nearest beach parking lot and pulls her journal out of her computer bag. She stares at the waves for a few minutes and then begins to write.

Dear Josie… Whoa… Shannon was asking some really deep and dark questions today. Questions about how I feel physically…mentally…spiritually. Questions about how I feel when Blake is near me. This is so hard. I'm so confused about everything that is happening in my relationship with

Blake. And when I try to talk with friends about what's going on, no one seems to understand. No one sees my struggles. No one knows what it's like to be Blake Solace's wife 24/7. It's my own personal hell. Oh Josie…what should I do? Shannon is trying to help me learn about the traits of particular personality disorders. Even with new knowledge, I still don't know what to do. Guess I'll just roll with it until I can figure out a plan of action. Well, I better get back to the office. Thanks, Josie…

14

Money Talks: Part 1

While attending Blake's company picnic, a coworker accidentally tells Tali that Blake's engaging in high-risk investing behaviors with their paycheck funds. She also hears someone talking about Blake's recent harassment charge. While driving home from the picnic, Tali asks Blake about his investing activities.

He replies, "Oh, well, I've been researching some new investment strategies and talking with my buddies at work about their thoughts on investing, how they manage their own personal investment portfolios. It's all about asset allocation and stock diversification, honey. You wouldn't understand unless you want me to try to explain it to you in a way you could maybe understand." He lets out his shallow laugh that he does when he's being sarcastic.

Tali hates that little laugh. She says, "Sure, let's talk about your investing ideas. I would like to discuss putting aside some funds each month in addition to our company 401(k) plans to better plan for future retirement or a rainy day if one of us decides to retire early. I know that's a long way into the future, but I think we should discuss what types of investments we are currently into. Do you agree?"

Blake is squirming in the driver's seat as he replies, "Sure, of course. You sound like you've been doing some reading about investments."

"Yes, I have. A little. And I had the most interesting conversation with your coworker, Cord, who works in the risk management department at your company. He has some fascinating ideas about risk-return trade-offs and how he and his girlfriend are using some of their money from their paychecks to test some high-risk investing strategies currently to see what they can earn in the markets. Has he told you about his ideas?" She waits in silence and notices that Blake is starting to perspire a bit.

He says, "Yeah, Cord mentioned they were trying out something new. I don't know the details though. I'll ask him about it at the office on Monday. I'm curious now." He laughs shallowly. He pulls the car into the garage, and they each get out of the car. Tali goes inside, and Blake heads to the mailbox to check for mail while texting vigorously on his cell. The message reads, "What the hell did you say to Tali today? She's asking me questions about high-risk trading. She doesn't know shit about investing! What did you tell her?" He waits for Cord to reply.

Cord types, "I didn't tell her what you and I are doing, man. We just talked about what Jenna and I are investing in right now. Just the big picture. No details. Chill, dude."

"OK. She just went on and on about how we should look at our own investments. She wants to talk details with me. I need to hide some columns in my spreadsheet before she and I talk about this stuff. She wants to talk about future retirement and rainy-day plans. OMG," Blake texts.

Cord replies, "Wow. Good luck with that one. She seems smart. Let me know how it goes."

Blake grabs the mail out of the box and walks back inside.

Tali says, "Hey, when do you want to talk about investments? I'm in the mood now. Here's your computer. I'll make some coffee, and we can look at the spreadsheet you were so excited to show me the other day."

Blake stammers a bit. "Um…okay. Could we just sit for a few minutes? I need to relax after that picnic. You know how big social events wear me out. I'm gonna catch the end of the Southern Cal game and then we can talk." He sits down on his end of the leather sofa and grabs the remote to turn on the TV. Then he picks up his phone and scrolls through screens. He stops and taps to open his Google Sheets app as he acts like he is watching the game. As Tali passes the sofa, she sees he is in Google Sheets.

She says, "Oh, I left my laptop at the office yesterday. May I borrow yours—not your work one, the other one that's in the kitchen?"

"Sure," Blake replies. "Bring it here and I'll log in for you."

"Thanks," Tali says as she picks up his computer and walks it over to him on the sofa. He logs into Windows and hands the computer back to her. She gives him a kiss and takes the computer into the kitchen to sit at the island while she works. She's thinking about what Cord said earlier. She does a Google search on some of the investment names that Cord mentioned that he and Jenna are considering. Ads for brokerage firms continue to pop up as she is reading online reviews about some of the companies. She notices that Blake gets up to go to the bathroom, so she opens Google Sheets and sees his initials on a cursor prompt in one of the columns. Looks like he is in that same file while watching the football game. She screenshots that page and each tabbed page in the file. When she hears Blake opening the door, she closes the file and goes back to her Google search.

He strolls over behind her and starts rubbing her shoulders as he says, "Is the computer working okay for you? What are you working on?"

Tali replies, "I'm so intrigued about what Cord was talking about. I'm looking up some terms that he was using so I can talk more intelligently with you when we discuss our investments later today. You know, we should have Cord and Jenna over for dinner soon. Could you get her number from Cord for me?"

"Sure," Blake says reluctantly. "That would be nice."

"Great!" she exclaims. "Hey, I thawed out some steaks yesterday to cook sometime this weekend. Wanna grill out later and do dinner on the terrace while we talk? I'll make a salad and some guac. Oh yeah, and I have some fresh sourdough that Sydney brought us from San Fran yesterday."

"Sounds great," he says as he sits back down, picks up his phone, and continues rearranging his Google Sheet columns and renaming investment abbreviations. He's thinking, 'She's smart, but I'm smarter, and I'll guide her attention toward cells that don't really matter in the big scheme. She doesn't know how to manage cash flows and spreadsheets like I do. Nobody's as good as me with spreadsheets. She'll be so impressed when I show her how great I am and how well our investments are performing. She'll never understand what I'm talking about. I'll throw around some fancy, big words that will go right over her head. Cord probably hasn't told Jenna everything. So far, it looks like our new strategy is working.'

15

He's Flipping Switches

Later that day, Blake wakes up from a nap on the sofa where he fell asleep looking at his phone and watching a game on TV. Tali had turned off the TV and covered him with a blanket. It's now seven o'clock. She's in the kitchen making guac and chopping veggies for a salad. The scent of sourdough fills the air as the bread is warming in the oven.

"Hey," Blake says as he comes into the kitchen and approaches Tali to give her a big hug and a kiss.

"Looks like someone had a good nap," she says as they stand there hugging for a moment.

"Yes, guess I needed it. Those company picnics get me every time," he muses with a smile.

Tali smiles. She says, "Steaks are in the fridge. What seasoning do you want to use on the meat tonight?" He opens the spice cabinet doors, looks over his options, and says, "I think that Kona spice blend we got in Maui would be nice. What do you think?"

"Sounds good," she says as she squeezes some fresh lime juice onto the avocados in the bowl she's using to mix up the guacamole. Blake grabs a chip and tests it.

"That's so good!" he exclaims and reaches for another chip.

Tali moves the bowl out of his reach and says with a smile, "Wait a minute, bud. Let me finish making this. I haven't even added the red onion yet! It'll be ready after you go start the grill and season the steaks."

He grumbles a bit and gets a beer out of the fridge while he is getting the meat. "Do you want a beer?"

"No thanks," she says. "I'll have something with dinner. Could we open the Syrah that the Mountain Chalet Hotel sent us after our last stay?"

"Sure." He approaches the wine rack and finds the bottle of Syrah. After opening it, he decants the wine and sets it on the countertop to breathe. Tali gets two red wine glasses out of the cabinet and places them beside the decanter on the counter. She opens the oven to check on the bread and then goes back to the island to finish making the dip and salad. She thinks about how this evening is going smoothly so far.

After the steaks are done, Blake's rare and hers medium, she brings the tossed salad, guac, chips, and bread to the table. She has already set the table on the terrace with the beautiful set of placemats and cloth napkins that her childhood friend, Sami, gave them as a wedding gift. She brings some olive oil and balsamic vinegar out to the table for dipping the bread, and then she lights a candle. Blake serves the steaks and goes back inside to pour the Syrah. He comes to the table and hands Tali a glass.

He raises his glass to make a toast. She does the same. He says, "To my beautiful wife, who makes me look good." They gently clink glasses before taking a sip.

"Wow, this is nice," Blake says with emphasis on the "wow." She agrees and comments that the wine sommelier at the Mountain Chalet has excellent taste.

"I'll send him a thank you note," she says. "You never know, I could offer to do some interior designs for the hotel and get us an invitation to come back."

Blake frowns and says, "That's crazy talk, sweetheart. I'm sure they already have a world-renown decorator. I mean, did you notice how expensive everything was when we were there?" He laughs shallowly as he takes a sip of wine and looks off toward the view of the bay.

Tali looks down at her dinner, slowly losing her appetite, and takes a sip of her water. She changes the subject with, "You did a nice job with the steak."

He says, "Thanks. I tried something new with a basting marinade this time. Think my new method worked well with the Maui seasoning I used. Glad you like it."

They finish eating dinner. Tali only ate part of hers. Blake's earlier comments hurt her feelings, and she didn't feel like eating or addressing his comments with him. He would only get mad at her and yell or tell her she was being too sensitive and that he was only kidding. It would be a terrible way to end the evening if she mentioned anything to him.

They bring the dishes into the kitchen. Blake opens the dishwasher and tells Tali to empty the dishwasher while he cleans the grill outside. She obliges and then begins storing the leftovers. After she finishes, she goes back outside to get the table linens and take them to the laundry room. Jasper walks outside with her and gets distracted by the smell of the grill. Jasper hangs out near Blake and the grill. He has a few pieces of grilled fat that he is clearing off the grill tray. The pieces are cool. He says, "Sit," to Jasper. She wags her tail and immediately sits. He gives her a piece and pats her on the head. She lays down and waits for another piece. He says, "Oh, girl, you definitely know the treat drill. Here you go," and he gives her another piece and pats her on the head again. "That's all I have," he says as he shows her his empty hands. Jasper wags her tail and looks over at Tali.

She says, "I don't have anything," and shows Jasper her empty hands. Jasper goes back to licking the floor under the terrace table and then follows Tali back inside. While in the kitchen, Tali starts making some coffee. "Would you like some coffee while we talk about investments?"

He replies, "I'm not feeling the investments conversation tonight. I really don't have any energy around it. Could we talk about it tomorrow?"

"Sure," she says, thinking she just wants to get this conversation over with and find out what Cord was talking about at the picnic earlier that day. When the coffee is done, she goes to her studio to work on some drawings for a meeting she has on Monday.

16

He Can't Be Alone

About an hour later, Tali hears Blake call out, "Hey, where are you?" She opens the door and calls from the top of the stairs, "I'm upstairs working on some drawings for work."

"Oh, do you have to do that tonight? Can't you come down here and sit with me? We can watch a movie. You can pick it out," he says in a whiny voice.

She replies, "Okay. Give me ten minutes to finish a thought."

"Good," he exclaims and loads Netflix on the TV.

17

Money Talks: Part 2

Tali wakes up early and takes Jasper for a walk. When she gets back to the townhouse, Blake is waiting for her on the terrace with coffee, fruit, and bagels with her favorite cream cheese. He'd gone to their favorite coffeehouse while she and Jasper were in the park. His computer is on nearby while he sips coffee.

"Thanks, babe," she says. "This looks amazing!" He smiles and gives her a kiss as he serves some fresh fruit and spreads cream cheese on her favorite kind of bagel, lightly toasted just the way she likes it, of course. She takes a bite of bagel, closes her eyes, and smiles. She sips her coffee and looks out to the ocean horizon.

She thinks, 'He must be having a good morning. Hope it lasts. I don't want to make him mad today.'

Blake says, "Let's talk about those investments you're so interested in."

She replies, "Okay. Let me get my iPad so I can take notes."

"You don't need to take notes. It's all in a spreadsheet," he says.

"I'll just be a minute," she says as she gets up to go inside and get her iPad. She comes back to the table and sits down.

He loads Google Sheets and pulls up a file titled "Solace Financial Investment Strategy." After the file loads, Blake starts scrolling through sheets and clicking on tabs. "Looks like it's all here. I haven't looked at this file since last week," he lies. She remembers seeing him looking at it on his phone yesterday.`

"Okay," she says. "Let's start from the top of the file. Tell me what the column headings stand for so I understand what types of numbers are in each column." He explains as she takes notes and asks a few questions. Then she asks him to run down the first column with account names so that she can get a feel for how the spreadsheet is organized.

He does this. Then he says, "Now that you see the setup, let's review the investment categories, and I'll try to explain to you why we're invested in certain types of securities. I know this can be so confusing. There are no stupid questions. Feel free to ask me anything, and I'll try to help you understand."

She replies, "Thanks, babe. I really want to understand, but you are right. Investments can be quite confusing. Thanks for your patience with me." She smiles.

He smiles as he says, "At least you're cute when you're trying to act smart." He laughs shallowly. Tali's stomach turns as she tries to ignore his rude comment. He begins explaining their investment goals and the timing of the strategy that he has designed to help them reach specific financial goals, such as when to buy a house, when to start a family, and when to retire.

Tali stops him periodically to ask a question. He provides sufficient answers to her inquiries. She takes notes along the way and comments that she'll do some research on her own. When he gets to the tabbed sheet with the allocations of their bi-weekly net compensation and starts to explain the spending and investing patterns, she posits this question, "I've been reading some articles online about investing and matching cash flows with financial goals — for beginners. What are your thoughts on risk tolerance?"

He looks at her with a raised eyebrow, as Tali continues, "We should agree on deciding which securities are safe enough but still yield needed returns for achieving our financial goals. What are your thoughts on risk tolerance, and how do you consider risk when you invest a portion of our paychecks each pay period?"

Blake listens quietly, squirming in his chair as he thinks about how he is going to answer her question. 'What did Cord tell her? Does she know about the off-balance sheet option stuff? Although, even if he did mention any of that terminology, she wouldn't understand what types of risk he was talking about.' He opens his mouth to respond when his cell phone sounds. "Oh, sorry, honey, I better take this. I'll be right back." He walks inside as he says, "Hey, Cord. Sure. Now's fine. What's up?"

Tali sees Blake through the French doors pacing while he's talking on the phone. She hears him raise his voice but can't tell what he's saying. He's on the call for about twenty minutes. After he ends the call, Blake stands inside with the doors closed for a minute staring at his phone with a concerned look on his face. When he notices that she is looking at him, he smiles at her, opens the doors, and comes back outside.

He sits down and starts apologizing. "Sorry about that. Cord is at the office right now, and he's having a crisis with a project we've been working on for months. I talked him through it. He'll be fine. Now, where were we?"

She looks at him. His face is troubled, his eyes dark. "Are you sure everything's okay?" she asks. "Do you need to go help Cord?"

"No," he replies. "I told him you and I are reviewing our financials and told him to call me if he's still having problems with the allocation strategy we're implementing. The markets reacted a bit differently than we predicted on Friday. With the picnic yesterday and then he took Jenna out to a movie last night, he's just now looking at the results from the trades we did on Friday. We had a staff meeting on Friday afternoon right after the markets closed, and we didn't review any outputs like we typically do at market close each day. He's working on the report right now."

"Okay," she says. "You seemed upset while you were talking with him."

"Nothing for you to worry about," he tells her. "Now, your question about risk perceptions…" Blake continues to talk.

Tali's mind wanders, but she poses a few more questions. After about ten minutes, she says, "That makes sense."

"It does?" he asks her. "Really?"

"Yes, it really does," she says. "I'd like to ask a few more questions though."

Blake's eyes darken as he thinks about how to respond. "Oh, man. I'm tired of explaining all this stuff to you. You don't quite understand. You're making my head hurt. We can talk about this more later." He gets up from the table and goes inside, slamming the French doors, leaving her outside sitting at the table with all the breakfast foods and dishes for her to bring inside by herself.

'That's okay,' she thinks. 'I did ask too many questions. He's right to be frustrated with me. I'll let him cool down, and then I'll make a nice lunch for us later. Everything will be fine.' She begins the task of bringing the breakfast leftovers and dishes inside and putting the dishes in the dishwasher. Blake is nowhere to be seen. She notices that Jasper's leash is gone. Blake must be taking the dog for a walk. She returns to the terrace and sits at the table with her coffee and her computer to work on her presentation for work tomorrow. Misty jumps up into the chair beside her, sensing that Tali needs her company right now.

18

Mask Is Slipping

lake walks Jasper vigorously to the park while he talks with Cord on the phone. He screams, "What the hell were you thinking? Did you tell Tali about the options deal? That's just between us, dude!"

People nearby stare at Blake as he screams into the phone. He notices the expression on a young mom's face as she picks up her toddler who is running in Blake's direction toward the sandbox. Jasper always likes to run around in the park and play fetch with one of the tennis balls she usually finds in the sandbox. Blake tries to manage Jasper, while the mom and her toddler have turned away and hustle away from Blake and the sandbox, heading toward the swings. Blake forces a smile and then lowers his voice to continue speaking with Cord. He says, "I can't talk here. Let's talk about this in the morning when I get to work. What time are you getting in? Okay, I'll see you then." He ends the call. Jasper finds a ball in the sandbox and brings it to Blake to throw. They play fetch for a while. When the sun is directly overhead, Blake glances at his phone and sees that it is lunchtime.

'Jasper must be ready for some water, and I'm hungry,' he thinks. They walk back home. Jasper happily laps water from her water bowl when they enter the laundry room for Blake to put away her leash and remove his shoes.

When they return, Tali is in the kitchen making chicken salad with vanilla yogurt, celery, and dried cranberries. Blake loves her chicken salad. She fills her water glass and gets a glass for Blake. He thanks her and goes into the family room. After a few minutes, he says, "Hey, what do you want to do for our autumn trip? It would be fun to plan another adventure for after our anniversary trip. I can't wait to take you to San Fran and Napa, Tali! We're gonna have so much fun! Want to go to Tahoe when the leaves start turning?"

She enters the family room with a plate of chicken salad sandwiches and some of the fresh fruit from breakfast. Returning to the kitchen to get their water glasses, she adds a slice of lime left from making the guac the previous night.

He says, "Wow! I love your chicken salad! Thanks. You're the best." He smiles at her as he takes a bite of his sandwich.

She says, "Sure thing. Tahoe sounds nice. Do you want to visit Tiff and Daniel while we're there? Aren't they like 45 minutes from Tahoe?"

"Good idea," he says. "Sure, call Tiff and see when they'll be around. Would be good to see them. I haven't seen Dan since the wedding. Didn't you have dinner with Tiff at that design conference in Boca last spring?"

"Yes, but there were like twenty of us at dinner that night. Not quite the setting for talking and catching up with an old friend. I can't wait to get together with them. I'll call Tiff after lunch." Tali pauses. Then she adds, "Are you doing okay? I seem to have upset you earlier."

Blake scoots closer to her as he says, "I'm fine. It's just that project with Cord and everything going on at work. Jasper took me on a walk and made me play fetch with her with another tennis ball she found in the sandbox at the park." He reaches down to pat Jasper on the head. She's lying on her side, and her wagging tail waps the rug as Blake pats her head. They finish eating lunch, and Tali clears the plates and takes them to the kitchen. She stores the leftovers and loads the dishwasher. Then she goes up to her studio to call Tiff.

Tali dials Tiff's cell and is delighted when Tiff says, "Hello?"

"Hi, Tiff! It's Tali!"

"Wow! Dan and I were just talking about you. Have you got ESP or something?"

"Should my ears be burning?" Tali jokes. They both laugh.

Tiff says, "I read the article about that new design your firm did for the Chamber in Newport. Looks amazing!"

"Thanks," says Tali. My boss, Sydney, led that project. She's a very gifted designer. I feel blessed to be working for her." The two friends continue their conversation with updates on Tiff's latest design project and then about a possible autumn visit.

Meanwhile, Blake calls Daniel. "Hi, Dan," Blake says when Dan answers. Blake tells Dan that Tali needs a trip away from the stress of work. He says he fears for Tali's mental health under the stress. Tali overhears him but doesn't let him know this time that she overheard him lying about her. After tiptoeing back to her studio, she opens her journal.

Dear Josie… I just heard Blake talking with our friend Dan about me. His words make him sound like he's concerned about me, but he's lying to our friends, telling them that I'm having mental issues and that he fears for my sanity. He told Dan that my job is too stressful for me. It's not! I love my job! Is Blake projecting his own insecurities about his job onto me? I wonder…

19

Laundry Duty

Blake demands that they do laundry each Sunday afternoon. Today, they're folding clothes while watching a pro football game. Tali would rather watch the golf tournament, but Blake won't let her play golf or watch golf anymore while he's around. So, they watch whatever he wants to watch during laundry duty every Sunday.

Suddenly, Blake screams, "You are not good at anything, Tali! You can't even wash my socks without getting lint on them! Look at these!" He holds two socks in her face. "I'm banning you from ever touching my laundry again!" He storms out of the room carrying two laundry baskets.

About an hour later, Tali hears Blake talking to someone in the master bedroom. He's Face Timing with his older brother, Thomas, while he steams his khaki pants. He's telling him all about his new research on the best laundry techniques and about the new state-of-the-art lint roller brush that he ordered on Amazon. "It should arrive tomorrow! I'll call you tomorrow evening after it gets here so I can show you how amazing it is!" His brother responds with a shallow laugh…a familiar sound.

20

Under the Radar

Blake arrives at his office building at 8 a.m. sharp. It's Monday after the company picnic. He stores his briefcase in his cube before heading over to Cord's cube. 'Cord looks rough,' Blake thinks. "How's it going?" he asks.

Cord looks up at him with bloodshot eyes. "I've been working on the computer since we talked yesterday morning. Jenna made me stop for dinner last night. I did take a break this morning to shower. You're welcome. And I've been here since 5:30 this morning talking with people in the India office and trying to figure out what happened on Friday. This is bad, Blake," Cord says, lowering his voice. "Not only did we crash the returns for the project, but we tanked the options strategy on our own portfolios. Did you explain everything to Tali yesterday? She seemed to know something was up."

"Hell, no," Blake whispers. "She can't know that I've lost a whole month's worth of pay. We'll make it back. Does Jenna know?"

"No way," Cord whispers back. "We need a comeback plan… and fast."

"We'll figure one out," Blake says. "Just stay calm. First things first. We need to figure out how to reinvent the investment strategy for our asset allocation project. What did the India office have to say about Friday's options market returns?"

"They have some theories, and they're calling me back in about an hour. I'll come get you to join the call in the Suite B conference room. I already reserved it. I think this conversation needs to happen behind closed doors. When we save this deal and earn sustainable income streams for the firm, we should be getting our own offices." Cord's voice trails off as their boss appears to be walking in their direction.

Their boss, Adam, smiles as he approaches the two men chatting in Cord's cubicle. "How are you two this morning? Looks like you're in a deep conversation. Anything you want to share?" Adam inquires as he crosses his arms and leans lightly against the cubicle's entry frame. Blake and Cord look at each other as Blake answers, "Just talking theories, that's all. Brainstorming for the next leg of the asset allocation project." Cord nods.

Adam says, "That's good to hear. I enjoyed talking with your significant others, Tali and Jenna, at the picnic on Saturday. They are lovely and very smart ladies. How they decided to hook up with you two, I'll never understand." He smiles and waits for their reply.

"Very funny," Blake muses. "Cord and I…we're great catches. One day soon, boss, you'll agree." Adam laughs heartily as he strolls away. He calls out, "Blake Solace, you're always handy for a good laugh."

Later that day, after the conference call with associates in India, Blake and Cord remain in the conference room to talk privately about their dilemmas regarding their asset allocation project for the firm and their own personal investing quandary. They emerge from the conference room with a new perspective and new ideas for diffusing their situations. First, they go to Blake's cube to log into his computer and add today's market movements to his project model spreadsheet. Then, they load the options trading floor application and observe the activity. They remain silent as they await the outcomes that their India counterpart predicted when they spoke earlier. As the India markets close, the options prices begin to behave per their colleague's expectations. Blake and Cord share a sigh of relief. They record the upward trends in Blake's model spreadsheet and agree to meet first thing tomorrow to continue the tracking and recovery. They text their colleague in India with appreciation and schedule a time to conference tomorrow after the U.S. markets close. Affirmation arrives from the India office.

21

Harassment Charge?

An hour later, Blake sits at his desk looking over his and Tali's investment portfolio spreadsheet and adding updated options values. He thinks things are not as bad as they seemed to be this morning.

At that moment, Adam appears in his cube with a manager from Human Resources. "Blake, we need to talk. Let's go to my office now."

"Okay," he replies. The three of them walk to Adam's office. Adam opens the door and motions for Blake and Hillary Dansfield, VP of Human Resources, to enter. Hillary takes a seat across from Adam at his desk, and Blake sits down in the chair beside Hillary.

Blake is nervous. He doesn't think this feels like a positive situation.

Adam opens the meeting with, "Blake, Hillary came to me with some disturbing news about you. I hired you, and I am viewing this news as conjecture and hearsay until I learn something different from you or from those purporting these behaviors. Hillary, please share the allegations with us."

"Thanks, Adam. Blake, I'm the messenger here. One of your employees came to me and shared some concerning information about you. And, on the same day last week, Adam's boss, Jennifer Paget, came to me with the same concerns after hearing about your comments aimed at a female coworker during a meeting with fifteen team members in the Suite C conference room last Wednesday. Can you confirm your attendance at that meeting?"

"Yes, the standing Wednesday noon meeting with associates in the Investments and Risk Management departments. Of course, I was there. I never miss that meeting."

"Okay, then, good," Hillary says and types some notes on her laptop. "So, one of your direct reports and Jennifer reported to me that you made a gender slur toward a female participant—not once but twice—during that meeting. Do you recall such behavior on your part?"

Blake shrugs his shoulders and says, "I don't recall what I could have said that would have been perceived as a gender slur. Did they tell you what I said?"

Hillary replies, "Yes. Your comments are documented, and actually, that entire meeting was recorded on Zoom because the meeting host wanted a record of the meeting for future reference. I haven't listened to the recording. Adam and I want to give you the opportunity to explain your comments before we take this matter further up the ladder. But, if you don't recall what you said, I'll have to request a copy of the recording. Thanks for sharing your comments. We will contact you tomorrow to discuss the potential implications of your recorded comments. I'll call you later after I listen to it. Thanks, Blake. You may return to your cubicle."

Blake stands and starts to say something to Adam. Adam waves him off and makes the 'give me a call later' signal with his hand raised to his ear. Blake takes the cue and leaves the office as Hillary remains in Adam's office to talk for a few more minutes.

Blake heads back to his cubicle but instead veers over to talk with Cord about what just transpired in Adam's office. "Cord, you were at that meeting in C last Wednesday at noon. Did I say anything offensive during the meeting? I got chastised and accused by HR of making gender-offensive remarks to a female participant in that meeting, and one of my direct reports was there and also went to HR to complain about me."

Cord stares at him with widened eyes and says, "Whoa, man. Maybe it's that new chick they hired in accounting. You know, the blonde with the Ph.D. who's doing a case study comparing West Coast and East Coast investment firms. You were a little short with her when she questioned you about your Euro-options comment. You think it was her?"

"Could be. I don't know. Think maybe I should just bow out of this place while I'm still kind of okay with management. Except for you, people here don't like me and definitely don't respect me or my intelligence. I should leave."

Cord replies, "Yeah, maybe that's your best option. And maybe I should go, too, since the shit's about to hit the fan on the India options deal."

"No, you should stay. We can get that mess wrapped up by tomorrow, I think. And then you can take the bows and get the glory for the unprecedented yields on this new style of asset allocation plan."

"Okay, if you think so. Let's see where the chips fall tomorrow when we talk with India. Five our time tomorrow morning, right?"

"Yes, can't wait. Bring lattes with extra shots," Blake demands with a smirk.

22

Just Stop Talking.
You're Making My Head Hurt.

That evening at six, Blake sits on his end of the leather sofa with his laptop and a beer in a navy blue Yosemite koozie when Tali gets home from work. Jasper jumps up from her nap on the rug in the family room and runs to greet Tali with wags and kisses. Misty purrs quietly, stretched out on the hearth room floor. Her tail moves lightly. Tali welcomes the attention, and then she walks into the family room.

"Hey there," she says to Blake.

He looks up from his computer and says, "Hey, how was your day?"

"Good. How was yours? You're home early." She waits for his reply.

"It was okay. I think it's time to move on and find another job. They just don't like me, and now they're questioning my ethics, etiquette, integrity—whatever you want to call it. I'm done with them."

"Oh no. What happened?" she inquires.

"Tali, you're asking too many questions, and you're making my head hurt by you being here right now. I really don't want to talk about it. Can it wait? I have a call with a recruiter in twenty minutes. I'm trying to finish updating my resume to send to her before we talk. We can talk about this later. You know I can't multitask," he says with anger rising in his tone.

"Sure thing. Let me know if I can help," she says as she and Jasper leave the room for the kitchen. She opens her journal and writes.

Dear Josie… Blake has decided to quit his job. I'm not sure what happened with him at work today. I need to talk with Shannon. Hopefully, I can get an appointment for tomorrow.

Tali texts Shannon's assistant to request an appointment with Shannon for tomorrow.

23

The Ayes Have It

Tali was able to get a return appointment for ten the following morning. As Amy ushers her back to Shannon's office, Tali takes a now familiar seat in the recliner. Shannon gathers her notes and files off her desk and sits down in the side chair by the prerequisite client recliner many therapists have as standard in their offices.

"Hi, Tali. How has your week been?"

"It's been somewhat tolerable, with a few flare-ups from Blake," replies Tali. "Last night, he said he's quitting his job, and he won't tell me why."

"How did you handle the news?"

"He told me to go away because I was asking too many questions and I was making his head hurt just by being there. So, I said, 'Okay,' and left the room. Was that the right thing to do?" Tali is close to tears. "I just want to help him get through whatever he's dealing with right now. I still love him. I know he had some kind of depression in college because of his controlling/manipulative mother's emotional abuse, and he's been depressed off and on during the past few years. He's always trying to impress his mom. I always thought I could help him heal. I've noticed that when Blake talks with his mom or his older brother, Thomas, his mood changes. He becomes very sad and somber. I usually try to distract him afterward with a stroll on the beach or a nice meal. It's hard sometimes to bring him out of the funk caused by his family. It can be quite challenging. I'm an empath, Shannon. I care. I want to help him."

"I know you do," says Shannon. "But first, we need to get you mentally stronger so that you aren't hurt by his mental abuse. Then, we can work on ways to possibly help Blake. Let's build your coat of armor so that you can deflect his arrows and protect your Glad and Gloomy switches. Agree?"

"Yes," says Tali. "Let's do this."

"To get started, I'm going to throw out some random personality traits and ask you to give me your initial reaction, yes or no, if this describes Blake in his interactions with you or with others.

"Does Blake try to isolate you from being with your family and friends?"

"Yes. He acts very possessive and jealous when my family and friends are visiting. When they call, he yells comments from the other room while I'm trying to talk with them."

"Does Blake have an exaggerated sense of self-importance?"

"Yes. He always says that he's the smartest person in the room and everyone should recognize that fact."

"Does Blake accuse you of being the cause of his bad behavior?"

"Yes. Whenever he has a bad day and takes out his frustra-tions on me, he always brings it around to being my fault… Not sure how he always comes to that conclusion."

"Does Blake think people are jealous of him?"

"Yes. He thinks everyone wants to be just like him."

"Does Blake only care about his own desires and needs?"

"Yes. It feels like my only role in his eyes is to cater to his desires and needs."

"Does Blake manipulate others to get what he wants?"

"Yes. I'm starting to get a better picture of some of his work-ing relationships after hanging out with some of his coworkers at the recent company picnic."

"Does Blake criticize you in front of others or behind closed doors?"

"Yes. He does both."

"Does Blake have periodic unpredictable rages or cruelty?"

"Yes. Then he tries to make up with me by bringing me flow-ers and gifts and buying me nice dinners."

"Does Blake have tormenting behaviors, such as purposely causing fear?"

"Yes. When he rages at me, his eyes become almost black. It's scary."

"Does Blake become angry if you do not acquiesce and agree with him?"

"Yes. I've learned to tell when his emotions are starting to escalate, and I can sometimes pivot the conversation into a more pleasant interaction, but not always."

"Does Blake lack empathy for others and not tolerate other people's feelings or needs?"

"Yes. He doesn't seem to even know how to empathize with someone or even try to understand other people's feelings or needs. He only cares about himself."

"Does Blake have a high opinion of himself, a huge ego?"

"Yes! Definitely!"

"Is Blake often arrogant and condescending to you and others?"

"Yes. He talks condescendingly and makes snide remarks and then does that little shallow laugh when he says something hurtful to me or someone else."

"Does Blake refuse to acknowledge guilt or apologize for inflicting emotional pain?"

"He always blames someone else for whatever happens. He'll sometimes offer a kind of fake apology…like when he's trying to apologize to me for his rages. Like I mentioned earlier, he brings me flowers, gifts, fancy dinners."

"Does Blake take advantage of others for his own gain?"

"Yes. Every interaction with another human being has to benefit him in some way."

Shannon looks at Tali and says, "I think the Ayes have it. Our hour is up for today and, as usual, I have another client waiting. Ask my assistant, Amy, to make a two-hour appointment for next week. I'll be ready to share with you what I think you are dealing with. Okay?"

Tali doesn't know whether to be happy or sad, so she mumbles, "Thank you so much," and exits Shannon's office.

24

The Laugh

Stopping at the beach parking lot on the way to the office, Tali writes:

Dear Josie... Shannon is helping me to build a tool kit to manage someone with controlling manipulative behaviors. This is so hard. I still love Blake. I want to help him. But I don't think that's possible since he doesn't think he needs any help. He thinks he's perfect and everyone else around him needs "fixing." He and his older brother, Thomas, spend hours on the phone every week talking about what's wrong with everyone in their lives. They say such judgmental, mean comments, and then each laugh with that same shallow, little laugh... That laugh makes me sick every time I hear it.

25

The Boat

"It's time to get up and get going!" Blake yells at Tali. It's six o'clock Saturday morning. Blake takes control of making lunches for everyone going on the boat trip they are taking with two other couples, even though Tali is quite the chef. Blake commands Tali to gather towels for everyone and pack the ice chest with ice and waters and get Jasper's dog bowl, leash, and poop bags.

Tali is thinking, 'Boat trips aren't fun anymore. It's always all about Blake playing Captain and ordering everyone around all day. I feel sorry for our friends who are joining us for this trip to the lake. They're about to see more of Blake's ways than they ever have. Oh, well. My job today will be to buffer Blake's antics, as usual. I'm so tired. I wish we didn't have to go. Maybe it will rain and thunder when we get there, and we can just come back home.'

The two couples arrive at Blake and Tali's townhouse to ride with Blake, Tali, and Jasper to the lake. Blake is yelling at Tali then asks other people to help hook up the boat to the Jeep because Tali is not capable (even though she has been doing this task every summer for her whole life—her family has always had a boat). When they get to the lake, Blake yells directives at everyone—who's to load the ice chests into the boat, who's to remove the chocks from underneath the boat trailer tires, who's to load the skis and sea biscuit into the boat, who's to load the ski vests into the boat, who's to load the towels into the dry compartments in the bow of the boat, who's to walk Jasper and then load Jasper and her water bowl into the boat. Blake is grinning ear to ear as everyone scurries to do his bidding. No one else is smiling.

"Okay, Tali. You go ahead and get into the boat. Jack will back the boat down the ramp and then park the trailer. Then you won't have to think so hard and try to jump into the boat when I pull it to the dock. Jack can do that better than you."

"But Blake," Tali says, "I always launch the boat and park the trailer. I've never had any difficulty with those tasks or jumping off the dock into the boat. What do you mean?"

Jack speaks up, "Hey, it's totally fine if Tali does this."

Blake says, "Jack, I'd prefer if you'd do it today. Let's give Tali a break."

Jack says, "Okay."

Tali decides not to belabor the point and does as Blake instructs. The other two couples (Jack and Renee, and Bruce and Maddie) look over at Tali with surprised expressions as Blake continues to pontificate about what a great boat captain he is.

As the sun is beginning to set and after a day on the water, everyone is ready to head home. Tali goes to the parking lot to retrieve the Jeep with the trailer. She backs down the boat launch ramp while Blake is yelling at her from his captain's seat on the boat. Their friends and people in surrounding boats and on the ramp all have concerned looks on their faces. Tali stays focused on her task and expertly maneuvers the trailer down the ramp and hooks the boat to the trailer. She safely pulls the boat up the ramp out of the water and drives to the parking lot where they can fully secure the boat and store the gear before heading home.

On the way home, they stop for dinner at a local diner. The dinner conversation is light. They load back into the Jeep. Tali drives them back to their townhouse while pulling the boat. She'll pull the boat to a marine maintenance shop on Monday before work to get some work done on the boat. As she nears their townhouse complex, Blake yells at her that she always turns on the turn signals too late. This is the intersection to the townhouse complex where they live, which she drives multiple times every day. Tali says nothing, continues driving. When they pull into the community parking area that residents can use for temporary parking of boats, Sea-Doos, etc., Blake tells her to back out of the parking lot and drive in straighter. Instead, Tali puts the Jeep in park, turns off the engine, and hands Blake the keys. He screams at her to repark it. Tali gets out of the car and opens the tailgate to begin unloading wet towels and ice chests and other items into the townhouse. Maddie grabs Jasper's leash and walks Jasper around the complex. The others help Tali unload the items from the back of the Jeep. Renee whispers to Tali as they carry in the wet towels, "Blake really treats you like dirt. So sorry you're having to put up with this. Call me later." She squeezes Tali's shoulder and Tali nods sadly.

After Blake falls asleep on the couch watching the football recaps on TV, she turns off the TV before she leaves on a walk to the tennis courts in their townhome complex. While walking, she calls Renee.

26

Dear Josie…

After her walk, she settles into her home office chaise and writes…

Dear Josie, I'm done. I can't handle being married to Blake any longer. His rages this weekend while we were at the lake with friends were unconscionable. I don't understand why he acts the way he does. I can't wait for the next appointment with Shannon. She says she has some theories on what's going on with Blake. I need some answers…soon.

27

He Says, "You're the Problem"

nother week passes. This Saturday morning, Tali has been working in her office at home on a new design project for the past two hours. She heard the door slam when Blake left the house to take Jasper for a walk about thirty minutes ago. "He should be home soon," she thinks. This new design project has kept her pretty busy each weekend for the past few weeks. Blake has acted more coolly than usual toward her since she began this project. He does not encourage her to try to become more successful at her job. But when he works weekends, she always has to be on standby to listen to his rants, encourage him, feed his ego, tell him he's great, massage his shoulders, bring him cold drinks, and prepare his meals.

Tali comes downstairs when she sees Blake and Jasper through the window. She greets them cheerfully as they enter the mud room. Jasper lunges for the water bowl as Blake gives

Tali a quick peck on the cheek. Blake grabs a glass out of the cabinet and fills it with ice and water at the fridge dispenser.

"How was your walk?" Tali inquires.

"Good," Blake replies. "I saw Aaron. He's the new neighbor who moved into the Reynold's house last month. I invited him and his family to come over next Friday to cook out. Sound good?"

"That could be okay if I finish this design by Friday. Otherwise, I'll be working late on Friday. The client wants to meet with me and Sydney next Saturday morning at his new resort. Let's play it by ear. Tentative plans for Friday?"

The color in Blake's neck reddens as his eyes grow dark. Tali sees this impending fit of anger and changes the subject.

"How about brunch on the terrace this morning? I have some smoked salmon, bagels, your favorite cream cheese, and some capers that I picked up at the market on my way home from work last night while you were at band practice. How was band practice, by the way?"

Blake responds to the question with, "It was fine. The band director was so impressed with me last night! My playing was brilliant! All the other trumpet players were so jealous of me when the director gave me the feature solo for the next concert. It was great! You'll come to the next concert, yes? I'll take you out to dinner after."

Tali looks at her calendar on her phone. "When is the concert?" she asks.

"Sunday, June 26th, at three o'clock," he says.

"I'm scheduled to be flying back from NYC that morning after the meeting. I should be back in time. I'll meet you at the concert."

"Oh, okay," Blake replies half-heartedly.

'Wow. He didn't yell at me this time,' she thinks. "Let's take these trays outside to the terrace."

"Okay. Would you like some coffee?"

"Sure," she says. Tali walks outside while Blake waits for the coffee to finish brewing, then he steps onto the terrace, closing the sliding glass doors behind him. Misty is staring at them through the glass door. Tali jumps up to open the door for Misty to come outside on the terrace. She says, "Misty must have smelled the salmon. Come on, little lady." Misty purrs as she slinks by Tali's feet and then jumps up into Tali's chair at the table. Blake still has an air of coldness about him. He sits across from her and schmeers cream cheese on a bagel. Tali sips her coffee and looks at him.

He looks up at her and, with a smirk, says, "What are you staring at?"

"I'm not staring, just looking at you. You seem to be disappointed in me these days. Having to work weekends seems to bother you, yet when you have a big project and have to work on a weekend, you expect me to be all nice and supportive, not judgmental and chilly like you're acting toward me right now."

Blake chomps on his bagel while listening to her. "I'm not judgmental or chilly. You're just overreacting like you always do. You always bring emotion into every situation, Tali. You have an overactive imagination. Nothing's wrong with me. You're the problem. Your self-esteem is pretty low. You are definitely making the most out of drawing those pictures. It's just that working weekends and not spending time with me and not visiting with new neighbors because of your hobby is not a good use of your time."

Tali's eyes begin to water.

"Oh, yeah, now you're crying. Tali, you are way too emotional," Blake says as he stares at her condescendingly and with condemnation.

Tali looks upward and away from him for a few seconds. "I'm not crying. Just thinking about what you said and how you said it. Do you realize that since I've been working on this design project these past two weeks, you haven't yelled at me once? Before then, you were yelling at me about something or other every day. What's changed?"

He replies, "Well, I was talking with this new lady in my department. She's young and beautiful. Anyway, I was telling her about our marital relationship. And I've decided that yelling at you every day is not the way to handle you."

"Oh, really?" Tali remarks as she captures his gaze and holds unadulterated eye contact.

He says, "Yeah!" then cluelessly goes back to piling smoked salmon onto his bagel.

28

Must Move. Again.

Blake gets on the phone each evening after dinner. Retreating to her own space, Tali stays away from him. She continues working on converting the extra bedroom into her art studio/office. So far, she has painted the walls and now she's working on the trim. Some of her friends and their spouses helped her install a fab fireplace, and she often opens the windows to hear ocean waves while she works on decorating the room. She is so excited to draw and paint in her new studio. Blake comes home from work early every day during the next two weeks and sits on the sofa with his laptop and a beer. Sometimes he invites Tali to join him, but more often not. She wonders if he's still planning to quit his job. He keeps coming home early and barely talks to her. Something is up. She thinks, 'Is he going to make me move to a new city if he quits and finds another job?'

29

Game Night

It's your turn. Roll the dice and move.

Friday nights are extra special in many American households. Parents wrap up intense weeks on the job, while children complete another week of school. Before the ascendancy of technological devices like smartphones and iPads, families would often play games following dinner such as Monopoly, Parcheesi, or Dominoes.

Tali and Blake's Game Night tradition began while they were dating. She remembers the many times they played Monopoly. Blake was always the banker and used the race car token, while Tali always played as the silver top hat. This was more than a game to Blake. It was a winner-take-all played by his rules that were occasionally made up on the fly to his advantage.

This night, Tali and Blake have invited over another couple to join them in a game of Monopoly. Tali knows the wife from working out at the gym. After they finish their takeout pizza,

Blake places the Monopoly board on the kitchen table. As banker, he distributes the starting cash position of $1,500 each. He sets the tokens out, including the race car and the top hat. Derek picks the horse, and Ellen picks the Scottie dog.

They each roll the dice to determine who will go first, which falls to Ellen. As the game progresses, she is amassing properties and placing houses and hotels. It looks like she's going to walk away with the game. Blake is obviously distressed and announces to Derek, "Tali and I would gang up on Ellen, but you need to make a plan to mess up her operations."

Derek is shocked and says, "Hey man, back off. This is only a game, not war!"

Blake then verbally embarrasses Tali, forcing her to form a united front to block Ellen's monopolies and prevent her from having an advantage. The game ends with Blake winning, but also alienating the couple who promptly leave for the night, never to return.

Later that evening, Tali complains that this is why they have no couple friends. "You are so competitive, and you get rude at the expense of winning at all cost. It's a parlor game — supposedly played for fun."

Blake ignores her and turns on the TV.

Dear Josie… Why is Blake so mean to my friends? My friends and their spouses don't want to hang out with us because each time they do, Blake either yells at me or says something mean to them. I feel sorry for Blake. He told me yesterday that the reason no one invites us over to their homes for dinner gatherings is because I am so gifted at entertaining that I intimidate everyone, so they don't want to invite us over. I don't believe that… I think it's because my friends' spouses don't want to be around Blake or have him in their homes around their families. He now says he has found a potential job in Monterey. I don't want to move. Let's see how his interview goes. I'll do what I can to help support and encourage him.

30

Gigabytes at the Beach

lake and Tali decide that they need to get away for a few days to work on their relationship. So, they fly to Florida to visit one of the beautiful white sand beaches. Tali stands at the edge of the surf on the shore at Pensacola Beach. She feels the sand gently eroding from under her feet as the tide ebbs and flows on the shoreline. It's late afternoon, and she sees dolphins swimming parallel to the beach as they seek their seafood dinner. Tali stares into the sunset. 'Is the sun setting on our marriage?' she wonders. Then she hears someone calling out to her. She turns around to see Blake heading her way with a smile on his face. She waves as she braces herself for whatever he wants to pontificate about this time.

He says, "Hey! Whatcha doing?" as he reaches for her hand and tugs her back up the beach toward the hotel. "Just thinking and watching the dolphins. That's all."

He says, "Yeah, I saw the dolphins this morning when I came out here at six this morning to tread water in the surf for an hour. My fit watch told me that I burned 660 calories in that hour, and my heart rate is better than ever. I'm so fit! You're so lucky that I'm in such good shape and could outlive the expected average male life span!"

Tali continues looking longingly out toward the waves. As they make their way up the boardwalk to their hotel beach entrance, they stop by the outdoor shower to rinse off their feet and legs. Tali rinses off the seashells she found on her walk, a sand dollar and a crimson scallop shell.

After the elevator delivers them to their floor, they walk to the door. Blake swipes the key card and opens the door, motioning for Tali to enter the room first. Once inside, Tali opens the fridge to get a cold water and offers one to Blake. He accepts. Then while Tali starts getting ready for dinner, Blake plops onto the sofa, turns on the TV, and opens his laptop. He scrolls through messages and reviews credit card charges. When he sees the mobile phone bill, he jumps up and runs into the bathroom where Tali is brushing her hair.

"We need to talk."

She says, "About?"

"I see here that your cell phone data usage increased since last month. What's that all about? You know you need to use Wi-Fi every time you can. Why did you use so many gigabytes? My data usage is so much lower."

"Don't you have a work phone?" she inquires.

"Yes, but that's not the point. You're using way too much data on your phone every month," he says as the volume of his voice increases. "I also noticed the grocery bill this past month was way higher than it should be for just us two. What's going on with your outlandish spending habits, Tali? I'm going to have to move money from our brokerage account again, all because of you. You need to start thinking about what you are buying and also only use your phone when you can get a Wi-Fi connection. Does that make sense?"

Tali listens then, after pausing, says, "Okay. I need to see the credit card statements so that I can see my spending patterns. This overspending doesn't compute. Let me see those statements now."

"No, not right now," Blake says. "We'll be late for dinner. We have seven o'clock reservations. We can talk about this matter later." Blake returns to the sofa. His thoughts are swiftly focused on how he can hide his expenses so that Tali doesn't see all the clothes and expensive bars and restaurants that he charged this past month. Tali emerges from the bathroom wearing her teal and white sundress. Blake goes into the bathroom to take a quick shower and get ready for dinner. He then goes out onto the balcony, where Tali has retreated. "I'm ready," he smiles, opening the door for her.

31

Airport Rage. Every Time.

Blake and Tali are enjoying the trip. They decide to spend an extra day touring the Gulf Coast and then take the red-eye flight back to Newport Beach. They turn in their rental car convertible and take an airport shuttle to the terminal. As Blake and Tali are riding in the shuttle, Blake says, "We need to finish our money-spending conversation when we get home. I'm really concerned about your spending habits, Tali. If we're ever gonna reach our financial goals, you need to overhaul your spending. I'm the frugal one. We'll talk about this further when we get home." He reaches to hold her hand as she stares out the window with tears in her eyes.

She has been reviewing their joint credit card statements for the past few months since Blake's erratic behavior has been escalating. He's been charging on their cards above and beyond anything she has spent. Blake has spent seven thousand dollars on new clothes for himself this summer so far. She has not. She wonders what he is trying to imply. Should she call him out on his spending patterns? Is he having an affair? No, he'll only try to deny or justify his questionable behaviors like he always does. It's not worth his rages and the battle to try to get to the truth.

They arrive at the airport. Blake instructs Tali to go to the kiosk and log her flight confirmation information. The kiosk is down, and an airline representative approaches Tali to explain the situation and offer assistance on checking in and getting her boarding passes. Blake steps between the flight representative and Tali and says that his wife is incapable of checking in by herself and he will handle it. Tali tries to tell him that the kiosk check-in system is down and the nice airline representative is trying to help her check in and obtain her boarding pass. Blake says, "Whatever," and storms off in a huff. Tali says to the flight representative, "I'm sorry. My husband has difficulties in airports. Thank you for helping me."

The flight representative replies, "I'm so sorry that you have to live this life and deal with him. I recently divorced a very controlling, manipulative man. I fell into the trap. Please forgive me if I'm overstepping my bounds. But I can see the signs. You seem like an intelligent, empathetic person. Don't let him control you and destroy your beautiful personality and love of life like I did. Here's my number if you ever want to talk. Hang in there." She hugs Tali then continues to help get her bag checked in and her boarding pass printed.

Blake is sitting in the chairs in the airline check-in area waiting for Tali. He stands up as she walks toward him, ready to enter the security queue before heading to their gate. They board the plane. Blake is a white-knuckle, stressed-out flier. While he adjusts his seat and stares at the flight online movie screen, Tali opens her journal and writes.

> *Dear Josie… Blake and I are on the airplane flying home from our trip to Florida. The trip was nice… Walks on the beach were breathtaking… Beachside inn was cozy. I enjoyed talking with the innkeeper and his wife. They are a very delightful couple who've been married fifty years! When we arrived at the airport today, Blake turned back into the raging Blake of recent months. He was so rude to the flight representative who was working to help me with the kiosk check-in when the kiosk went down. He let out a conceited huff as he stormed off away from me and the person helping me. Why does he act this way? Am I doing something to set him off? I can't figure out what I should do.*

32

Similar Personalities

Tali and Blake arrive in California after the red-eye flight from Florida. Upon returning home, they settle into the townhouse, and Tali picks up Jasper and Misty from Molly's house later that morning. She heads to the yacht club at noon to meet up with Sydney and a new client. Sydney motions Tali over to the table when she sees her enter the beach bar area.

"Tali, this is Gordon Silvers, commander of the yacht club, and he is vice president of the nonprofit Assurance Messengers who educate consumers about the dangers of illegal drug use. He also manages a venture capitalist firm that invests in ecological sustainability programs. He would like to hire our firm to redesign the interior spaces of the yacht club."

"Hello, Mr. Silvers, it's a pleasure to meet you. I read your latest book. Fascinating statistical analysis of the efficacy of legislation on mitigating the use of illegal substances in this country. Do you believe your research and proposed legislation could have a global domino effect?"

Sydney smiles as they await Gordon's response.

He says, "Why yes, I do, Tali. I'm impressed that you know about my work in this area. Did you know that I'm also a famous journalist, and the legislation that I proposed and got passed last year reduced illegal substance fatalities in sixteen states this past quarter?"

Tali replies, "Wow! No. I didn't know that."

"Well, now you do," says Gordon.

Sydney says, "Tali will be leading this redesign project. Would you like to give us a tour of the yacht club so we can take a few pics and start brainstorming some ideas for your spaces?"

"Yes, of course. Right this way, ladies." Gordon opens the door and motions for them through the doorway into the dining room.

*****

As Tali begins working with Gordon Silvers, she quickly notices his need to control situations. During their first lunch meeting to review her preliminary sketches, he tells the hostess which table to seat them at in the yacht club café. Then he orders drinks for them both without consulting Tali. He then tries to order Tali's meal, but she interrupts him at that point and tells the server her lunch preferences after inquiring about the details of a few menu options. During the meeting, Gordon continues to brag about his superior intellect and achievements. Tali has learned from being married to Blake how to redirect a conversation. She leads Gordon into a conversation about what he and the yacht club board envision for the ambiance of the new clubhouse atmosphere. Gordon appears a bit startled that such a young lass like Tali can change the direction of this meeting so eloquently and efficiently. The meeting concludes after an enlightening conversation. Tali has many notes on her sketches to consider and implement before their next meeting.

She calls Sydney on the way back to the office. "OMG, Sydney, Gordon's just like Blake. He has the same controlling personality. You gave me this client as a joke, right?" Tali muses.

Sydney replies, "Tali, I'm so sorry. I didn't realize how he was. I had only spoken with him briefly before I introduced you to him. I can reassign someone else to Gordon if you don't want to deal with him."

"Thanks, but no. I can manage Mr. Silvers. I've been building a tool kit for handling difficult, controlling personalities. I look forward to the challenge… I think."

"Well, know that I've got your back and I'm here for you if he gives you any trouble," Sydney adds.

Tali says, "Thanks, boss… You're the best."

33

Just a Band-Aid

"Hey, Ash!" Tali shouts while heading toward the softball field. Ashley is limping toward the dugout.

"Hey, Tali," Ashley replies.

"Oh no. What's up, Ash?" Tali asks.

Ashley replies, "I was working out yesterday, and I think I twisted my left knee, or maybe I irritated that old college soccer injury. Pretty painful. I need to pitch for the company team today though. Blake pretty much threatened me when he heard that I might be out of the lineup today. He doesn't believe me about my college knee injury and the three surgeries that ended my soccer career. Ever since he became coach of this company team…OMG. Sorry, I shouldn't complain about him. He's your husband."

Tali says, "Ash, please, feel free to talk frankly with me. If you're hurt, then we'll find someone else to pitch today. Let's get some ice for your knee. Here, let me help you." Tali picks up

Ashley's bat bag and holds her shoulder as they walk together toward the concession stand to get ice for Ashley's knee. While they sit on the bleachers before the game begins, Ashley shares with Tali Blake's work demands. He has asked Ashley to cover for him on a project even after she'd already been given time off this coming week to go home for her mother's cancer surgery. Blake raged at Ashley. "He told me, 'I'm more important than your mother.'"

After talking with Ashley, Tali is wondering why Blake disregards everyone else's challenges and injuries/hurts.

Dear Josie… while I was at the softball game today, Ashley confided in me how mean Blake is as he's coaching the company softball team. He forbade her to take time off to be with her mother who is battling cancer. What is going on in Blake's mind? I can't talk with him about Ashley because then he would know that she confided in me and then he would rage at her. Oh, Josie… I need to learn how to handle Blake's chaotic behaviors…and help others learn how to manage him and his violent/traumatizing outbursts.

34

Tires

Tali's tire treads are bare. Tali slips and slides on barely wet roads. She tells Blake when she arrives home after grocery shopping on Saturday morning, "My car is not handling properly. The tire treads look too worn. And the brakes are spongy. I'll call the tire place today and schedule a time this week to get new tires."

Blake replies, "They're probably fine. You always exaggerate everything, Tali. I'll go measure the treads right now." He grabs some change off the counter desk where his wallet lays as he exits the kitchen and heads to the garage. In the garage, he places a dime into each tire's tread line. He soon returns to the kitchen and announces, "Your tires are fine. Plenty of life left in them. No need to call the tire place."

"How do you know?" Tali asks.

"I tested the depth of the treads with a dime. They look fine," he replies.

She says, "Well, it was pretty scary slipping on barely wet roads today on my way home from the store. I'm gonna get them checked out this week anyway by the experts at the tire place."

He replies, his voice escalating, "Okay, whatever. You don't think I'm smart enough to test a few tire treads?"

"I didn't say that. I only want to be sure that nothing's wrong with my tires. It's a safety issue. I'd feel better if I knew for sure," she says.

Blake slams the garage door, thinking to himself, 'Her tires are perfectly fine. It's just that she's a bad driver and not braking soon enough. It's not the tires. It's her fault, of course.'

Tali is inside thinking about the conversation and Blake storming out of the room. 'I was trying to talk calmly and not make him upset. Doesn't he care about my safety? Guess not. Getting a free evaluation at the tire place this week is a must.' Tali heard recently that today's standard to measure tire treads is using a quarter, not a dime anymore. 'I need a professional evaluation. I don't trust Blake anymore.'

She calls to schedule a free evaluation at the tire place near her office.

On Monday, Tali goes to the tire place on her way to work. Her friend who works there tests her tire treads and tells her that just looking at the tires, anyone could tell that it's past time for new tires. Tali takes photos of the tires. She orders new tires and then schedules a time to install them later in the week. Tali leaves there with a new sense of confidence that she made the right call, even in the wake of Blake's rage.

Later in the week, her friend at the tire place calls her to tell her that four new tires arrived a day early and asks if she could bring her car over today. She agrees and then calls Molly to see if she has time to pick her up from the tire place after work and drive her home. Molly says she could do that and they could get dinner on the way home. Tali loves the idea and is very appreciative to have such a great friend in Molly.

The next day, her friend at the tire shop calls to tell her that her brake pads need to be replaced because they are too worn and the rotors are at risk of being damaged within the next few hundred miles if she doesn't get the brakes maintained now. Tali approves the repair.

When Blake hears about the brake repair request during a phone call with Tali that afternoon, he says nothing about it to Tali. Instead, he calls the repair shop to cancel the brake job, telling the repair shop owner that his wife doesn't know what she is talking about and the brakes on the car are fine, even though Tali told Blake that the brakes have been making a chirping sound consistently for two weeks and they have been spongy when she tries to use the brakes.

While Tali's car is in the shop, Blake texts her that her car's computer system notified him that her tire is deflated. He's the only one who receives the message because her car is in his name only. He convinced Tali that she is a terrible negotiator, so all marital assets—both cars and the townhome—are in his name only.

35

Packs Her Bags

Sydney drives Tali to the tire place to pick up her car on Friday evening after work. Her friend at the shop tells her that they didn't do the brake job because Blake called to cancel it and said that Tali doesn't know anything about cars and the brakes are fine. Tali is shocked! She tells them to do the brake job then schedules an Uber to go home.

Upon arriving home, she realizes that Blake is not home from work yet. She enters the townhome and receives kisses from Jasper. Misty wanders over and nuzzles against Tali's leg while she fills each pet's food dish and water dish. She adores feeling unconditionally loved by these two. While Jasper and Misty are enjoying their dinners, she climbs the stairs to the master suite and retrieves two duffel bags from her closet. She opens each bag and begins packing her clothes, toiletries, and her favorite stuffed animal. She is about finished when she hears the garage door open. She places her bags at the base of the stairs. She gets a couple reusable shopping bags from the pantry and fills each with some of Jasper's and Misty's toys, leashes, treats, and food. 'Blake must be on a phone call since he hasn't come in from the garage,' she thinks. She goes over to Jasper's dog bed and Misty's cat tree to retrieve their favorite blankets. She places the blankets into one of the bags and then sets the filled bags beside her packed duffel bags.

She texts Molly, "Hey. May I stay with you tonight? And the pets?"

Molly replies, "Of course! Come on over!"

"Thanks. My car's in the shop. Could you pick me up in about thirty minutes?"

"Of course," texts Molly. "See you in thirty."

Just then, Blake walks through the door. Jasper, Misty, and Tali are standing beside the staircase, duffels and bags at her feet.

He says, "How are my ladies doing? Sorry I'm a little late. Was on a business call. What's going on? Where's your car? I thought you were picking it up today after getting new tires."

Tali begins to speak while trying to hold back the tears, "I heard about you canceling the needed brake job and telling them I'm crazy. What the hell, Blake? What are you trying to do? This is the final straw—your rage and going behind my back telling my friends you think I'm crazy and incompetent. Why? I'm leaving for a while. I'm taking Jasper and Misty with me. We need some time apart to figure out what's going on with you and me." Her eyes are filled with tears.

Blake says, "No, don't leave," as he crosses the room to embrace her. Tali steps back, and Jasper and Misty stand in between them. "I'm sorry. I was only reaching out to people who know you to see if anyone else besides me has noticed that you're not quite working on all cylinders these days, honey. I want to help you. What can I do to help you, to help us? I want us to be together."

Tali replies, "Seriously? You yell at me every day, usually over nothing important. Why? I seem to set you off. I need to leave."

He says, "I'll stop yelling at you. It's just that work has been really rough, and then you seem to be doing so well at your job. Guess I'm jealous. Please let me try to make this up to you." He gazes at her pleadingly. She looks up at him, very concerned.

Tali says to Blake, "I'm leaving for a while. I'm done with your rages and fake apologies. The pets are going with me. They need a break from the daily drama around here too."

Blake says, "Don't go, Tali. I'll change." She determinedly sidesteps him as she says, "I have to go. Our relationship needs a break. I need time to think. *You* need time to think."

He says, "Well, you're just running away. You're as much to blame for our problems as I am. You're too emotional and too sensitive. Just like you've always been." His eyes are darkening as his voice decibels rise. Misty and Jasper scurry toward Tali… They know what's coming. Tali evades Blake's outreached hand as he tries to grab her arm. She steps toward the foyer to grab her bags and then quickly walks through the kitchen toward the door leading to the garage with Misty and Jasper following quickly behind her. Blake again says, "Tali, please don't go," as he tries to soften his tone… but to no avail. He's in a rage.

Tali presses the garage door button as she enters the garage. She sees Molly's car in the driveway. She and the pets rush toward the car as Blake follows close behind them, yelling, "Stop! Don't go. Molly, don't buy into Tali's lies about me!" Tali quickly opens the back car door to load the pets and her bags. Then she jumps into the front passenger seat and closes her door as Molly speeds away.

Molly says, "OMG, Tali… Are you okay?" while she slows to a stop at the next intersection as the light turns amber. Tali takes a deep breath and says, "Yeah… I think so. Thanks for picking up me and the pets."

"You're so welcome, girlfriend," Molly says as she studies Tali's face while they wait for the light to turn green. As the drive continues, Tali shares some details about the day: Blake canceling the brake job on her car and telling the mechanics that she's crazy… her decision to pack her bags… and her appreciation to Molly for rescuing them from Blake's fit of rage. Molly just listens and nods with an occasional "Oh no" and "Tali, I want to help you through this." They soon arrive at Molly's house, and Molly's husband, Chad, goes into the garage to carry Tali's bags inside. The two ladies bring Misty and Jasper into the house. Tali fills their water bowls and places the bowls in the mud room. Chad carries Tali's bags and the pets' blankets and toys upstairs to the front guest room.

Molly and Tali sit on the chaises in the hearth room overlooking the beach. The moon is full, and the waves are rolling into the shore. Tali stares out the window while Molly goes to the wet bar fridge and pours two glasses of Sauvignon Blanc. She walks back into the hearth room and hands Tali a glass. Tali says, "Thanks," and takes a small sip. She swallows slowly as she takes a minute to think about the experience she just endured. Her phone has been buzzing on silent mode with Blake's continuous texts and calls. She has not answered, and she's not planning to answer tonight. She needs time to think and decompress. "What have I done?" she asks, looking at Molly with wide, questioning eyes.

Molly replies, "You've done the right thing. He's been hurting you for quite some time. Leaving now is for the best. You need time away from him to think and decide your next move… and whether you want to try to work on the relationship or let it go. I'm here for you, friend."

Tali listens as she continues to look out the window. She replies, "I really think I'm done. I can't deal with any more of Blake's tantrums and rages. I'm done." Tears are falling. Molly puts her arm around Tali as she sobs. After a few minutes, Tali says, "I think I should go home to Mamita and Dad tomorrow. I need some time away. Back to my hometown. Time to step back and try to figure out what the hell I'm gonna do…what I should do. What do you think?"

Molly says, "I totally agree. How can I help? Would you like Misty and Jasper to stay with us for a few days? They love Reggie and Dandy. The pups and kitties would have a blast."

Tali says, "Yes. That would be awesome. They would have fun. I know I'm probably giving off stress signals to them right now. They always hide when Blake rages. They probably need some good calming time with their friends. Thanks so much."

"No problem. Happy to be here for you and your fam," Molly says with a smile.

Tali manages a small smile. She hugs Molly and thanks her again for hosting her and her pets this evening and for rescuing them today. Tali places her wine glass in the kitchen sink and then slowly ascends the stairs on her way to the guest room where Misty and Jasper have already retreated to their blankets on the guest bed. Chad had already unpacked the pets' blankets and toys and led them to the guest room while Tali and Molly were talking. 'What a great guy Molly has. He's so caring of everyone...even my pets. He always helps everyone feel so welcome in their home,' Tali thinks while watching the sleeping pup and kit. 'My friends are the best.'

The next morning, Molly makes coffee and cooks breakfast for Tali before she goes to work. Tali walks Jasper and feeds Jasper and Misty. After breakfast, Tali packs their bags then calls a taxi to get a ride to the rental car place. Upon arriving, she rents a convertible and starts driving home to Point Loma.

As she drives down the coast, she looks to her right to see the beautiful Pacific coastline and reminisces about times growing up in Point Loma. She can't wait to get home and spend time with her Mamita and Dad. She's missed them. She's been working long hours on top of all the time dealing with and trying to heal from Blake's rages. She pulls into her parents' driveway and sees her Mamita coming through the breezeway. She waves and motions Tali to pull her car into the back garage. Tali smiles as she pulls into the garage. She gets out of the car and hugs her Mamita as tears fall from her eyes.

Her Mamita holds her tight. "Aww, baby, I'm here. Just let it go. Let it out," Mamita says.

When Tali's tears slow, she shakily says, "Mamita...I need you. Blake has hurt me so badly... I can't take it anymore." She starts crying again. Mamita continues to hold her daughter tightly. After a moment, Tali loosens her hold a bit and looks at her Mamita. "I'm sorry. I know you and Dad didn't really like Blake. I married him anyway. I'm sorry..." Her voice trails off and she sobs again.

Mamita says, "Baby, it's okay. It's not your fault. Blake's rages and mean comments have been hurting you and beating you down for a while. *He's* the offender, not you, my dear."

"Thanks," says Tali. They enter the house and then retreat to the pool patio overlooking the beach. Mamita has fresh lemonade and a fresh fruits and veggies tray ready on the glass table beside the blue chaise. Tali pours some lemonade for each of them and then makes a plate of snacks before reclining on the chaise. They talk and laugh a bit while watching the surfers catch some midday waves. When they go back inside, Tali heads to the garage to get her bags and takes them upstairs to her room. She opens the French doors leading to her balcony and stares at the ocean view. She breathes in deeply…and reflects on her childhood. Her ringtone sounds and she sees the call is from Chelle, her best friend here since second grade.

"Hey, Tali! Thanks for letting me know that you're in town! How's life going? I'm sorry I haven't reached out in the past month. I've been in Paris on that new design job I told you about a few months ago."

"That's incredible, Chelle! I'm so excited for you! Can't wait to hear all about the new project! Would you have some time on Monday to meet up for lunch?"

"Yes! That would be glorious! Let's meet at the marina café at say one o'clock?" proposes Chelle.

"Sounds great! See you then! Au revoir."

Chelle replies, "Au revoir!"

Tali descends the stairs to the kitchen where Mamita is preparing dinner. "Hey! That looks good," she says.

"I'm making your favorite dish for tonight's dinner—fresh scallops. Thought you would enjoy it. Dad will be home in about thirty minutes. Would you like to start preparing the tossed salad? The quinoa is done. I roasted some corn on the grill."

"Aww... Mamita, you're the best!" Tali says as they hug. She goes to the fridge to grab salad ingredients. 'Mmmm...,' she thinks as she spies some fresh jicama and fresh banana peppers and, of course, her dad's out-of-this-world home-grown tomatoes. She's so happy to be home. She hasn't felt this happy in quite a while.

They decide to dine outside on the terrace overlooking the pool. Her parents both have concerned looks on their faces as she shares some stories about her marriage to Blake. She tells them about her sessions with Shannon and how much she is learning about individuals with Blake's personality disorder. They listen while they enjoy the delicious meal and interject supportive comments along the way as Tali unravels the mirage of a marriage she's been living with Blake. She talks with her parents every week, but she hasn't been able to share her struggles with Blake's tantrums and rages. She believed that she could help Blake work through whatever's going on in his mind and then they could live happily ever after, and no one needed to know the hard times they've endured during their still-young marriage.

On Monday morning, , Tali, Mamita, and Dad enjoy coffee with bagels and fruit before Dad heads to work as a commercial developer and Mamita has to leave for a meeting with a client for a newly commissioned art project. Mamita is a professional artist whom corporations commission to paint seascapes and landscapes for their lobbies, offices, and board rooms. A few times in Tali and Chelle's occupations as interior designers, clients have already commissioned Tali's Mamita to paint a masterpiece for their new spaces. Tali is so proud of her parents! After breakfast and telling her parents bye until later that evening, she calls Sydney and Molly. She updates each on her visit home. She and Sydney talk about work for a few minutes, but Sydney assures Tali that there are no tasks that must be completed this week. Tali appreciated her offer, but she did bring her computer and work files with her.

Early afternoon, Tali drives her convertible rental car to meet Chelle for lunch. During lunch, Chelle and Tali cover so much ground talking about each other's interior design projects and sharing ideas. Chelle's new beau is a professional chef who's currently studying in Paris while she's also been working on a design project in Paris. They update each other on their families, and then Blake's name comes up. When Chelle asks about Blake, Tali's whole body stiffens and her eyes tear up.

Chelle says, "Tali, I'm so sorry. I shouldn't have mentioned Blake. I didn't know it was this bad." She looks sympathetically at Tali, deeply concerned about her bestie.

"It's okay, Chelle. I've got to get to a place where I can be strong when I hear his name and not feel so PTSD by reflecting on the past four years of hell with that man. I still can't believe I dated him through college and then actually married the guy." Gathering herself, she continues, "I'm sorry. I've been seeing a counselor named Shannon. She's helping me sort through this mess with Blake and learn more about a particular personality disorder he seems to be exhibiting. It's a journey. I came home to sort out some stuff…some emotions…some logistics…and start figuring out a plan of action. Should I stay or should I go?"

Chelle listens and then adds, "Tali, I'm so proud of you for standing up to him and for coming home to family and friends who love you and will always stand behind you. How can I help?"

Tali replies, "Thanks, Chelle. Right now, I'm not sure what anyone can do. Bentley and I have been talking more often. My friend, Molly, in Newport Beach actually rescued me and my pets two days ago during one of Blake's rages. It was horrible. His eyes were nearly black as he ran after Molly's car. I've not talked with him since I left. Molly and her husband, Chad, are taking care of Misty and Jasper while I'm here. My boss and colleagues have been so supportive during this time of marital stress with Blake. She told me to not worry about work this week, though I'm going to work on a few projects tomorrow. Work is a solid escape and helps focus my mind when I start spiraling down with memories of Blake's rages and yelling sprees. Chelle, I appreciate you taking time out of your busy day to have lunch. I wish I had more pleasant news to share about Blake."

"Tali, seriously, I love you, girlfriend. We've been besties since second grade! Of course, I'm loving time with you! I want to hang out with you more while you're here this week!" Chelle says.

"Thanks, friend. You're so awesome. Yes! How about surfing on Saturday? I don't plan to drive back to Newport Beach until next Sunday."

Chelle says, "Sounds great!"

The two ladies switch to happier topics and catch up on more news while they eat lunch. As they reminisce and joke, their laughter is intoxicating. Tali feels a release of tension, as she begins to heal. After the long lunch, they hug and say so long until Saturday. When she gets back to her car, Tali drives to the beach. When she gets there, she puts up the convertible top, takes off her shoes, and grabs her sketch pad and pencils out of the front seat of the car. She ambles along the beach for a while and then sits on a rock near the shoreline. She opens her sketch pad to draw, losing herself in her art until her phone buzzes two hours later. It's Mamita texting to say that she's home from work and asking what time Tali would like dinner this evening. Tali texts back that she's finishing a sketch and will be home in about an hour. She says she'll help cook dinner when she gets home and tells Mamita that she loves her. About forty-five minutes later, she walks back to her car and drives home.

When she arrives, Mamita is in the kitchen. "How was lunch with Chelle and your afternoon?" Mamita inquires.

Tali says, "It was good catching up with Chelle. She's on a good life journey right now. Then I went to the beach to think and sketch."

"Oh, may I see?" Mamita asks.

"Okay…. But I'm not you, Miss Professional Artist," Tali says jokingly.

"Tali, it's beautiful!" Mamita says after Tali hands her the open sketch pad.

"Thanks. I still need to add some shading around the rock and wave spray. And the clouds were reflecting in the water over there," she says as she points to the upper righthand corner below the horizon line, "but it's a start."

"It's a great start!" Mamita says.

*****

Tali spends the next few days walking on the beach, sketching, talking with Mamita and Dad. On Saturday, she and Chelle hit the waves for a day of surfing followed by an evening beach volleyball game and a bonfire with some old friends. Tali's spirit and strength are renewed. She feels like herself again, instead of the beaten-down version of herself that Blake has forged in four short years of their relationship.

On Sunday morning, Tali enjoys breakfast with Mamita and Dad. They pack some food for her and help her pack the car for the journey back to Newport Beach. When she arrives at Molly's house, she is welcomed with open arms. Misty and Jasper are so happy to see her! She hugs them both as Molly helps bring her bags into the house. She stays the night there. She'll go to the office in the morning and then return the rental car and pick up her car with the new brakes during her lunch hour. After work, she plans to drive home to the townhouse. She feels revived, stronger, and more confident but is still uncertain about the conversation that she needs to have with Blake, especially when and how to confront him. She no longer believes it will make a difference but knows at some point she will have to.

36

Clears the Room

After Tali gets home, everything returns to normal — at least, their brand of normal. Tali is wary of being alone with Blake and plans gatherings as often as possible, starting with a small dinner party at their townhome the week after she gets back. During dinner, Blake makes rude comments and laughs shallowly after each dig at the people around the table. After dinner, Tali's friends gather around her in the kitchen to ask her about what's going on with Blake, telling her he seems meaner than usual.

Tali serves coffee and the dessert she got at their favorite bakery. Blake continues to say mean things to each couple until everyone is gone by 9:00 p.m.

Blake comments, "Everyone left earlier than usual this evening."

"You really know how to clear a room," Tali remarks.

"It's not my fault. You're the reason no one stayed."

Tali then recounts each set of comments Blake made to each couple and how he was the one who caused everyone to feel unwelcome.

Blake replies only with, "Hmmm," and then opens his laptop while perched on the end of the leather sofa.

Tali heads back into the kitchen to finish cleaning up and storing leftovers from the dinner party. As she is clearing up, she is deep in thought. Later that night, Tali writes:

Dear Josie… I'm not sure… I'm just not sure… I know I need to end this marital chaos…but how? Blake is disillusioned about the effects of his comments on other people. He literally cleared the room with his mean comments to each person in the room this evening. It was almost as if he were playing his own game…like he was trying to see how hurtful he could be before they would leave. Well, it's becoming evident that I might be next on the "need to leave" list. The trip to see my parents was golden. I'm stronger, but I still have a ways to go and quite a few more conversations with Shannon before I'm ready to pull the plug, if in fact that is what I need to do. Can this relationship be salvaged? I don't know if it can be. And then there's "that" night. The physical trauma is healed. The emotional trauma still looms inside me.

37

All the Rage

A month passes. Tali's physical cuts and bruises are healed from "her fall," as described by Blake. Blake is still trying to find another job. He has not told his boss that he is searching for another job. He has a phone interview for a potential job in Monterey on Wednesday morning. In the meantime, he is working through harassment allegations at his current employer. He still has not told Tali everything about the harassment charge. They go to a social gathering at his current boss's house.

"Thanks for a great evening!" Blake says to Adam and Lana, his wife, as he and Tali walk past the stone fireplace and through the elegant marble-floored foyer toward the front doors.

Tali and Lana share a quick hug as Lana says, "Tali, see you next week. I can't wait to talk with you!"

"Me too!" Tali replies with a smile. As soon as the doors have closed, Blake grabs Tali's left hand and pulls her aggressively to their car at the entrance to the circular drive. All other guests have already departed, so they have an open path to their car.

Tali whispers, "Blake, you're hurting me. Let go of my hand."

Once inside the car, Blake turns to Tali and screams, "What the hell were you thinking? You spent the whole evening talking with Lana! Not once did you come find me to see who I was talking to. How do I know that you didn't embarrass me? You probably did anyway. You always make friends with my co-workers' wives. Lana is my boss's wife, and you just met her. What on earth would you have to say that she would be so interested in? Oh, and what about her wanting to see you again next week? What the hell, Tali?"

Tali waits for Blake to stop ranting. She looks at him, noticing that his eyes are dark and distant. It's not the lighting in the car. Something is not right with him.

Blake's wondering whether anyone mentioned the harassment suit that he's keeping a secret from Tali.

She replies, "I'm sorry, I didn't know you wanted me to find you. I was only talking with Lana, Blake, I promise."

"I don't believe you," he rages. Blake starts the engine, forcefully shifts into drive, and speeds off. When out of sight of his boss's house, he pulls onto the shoulder and slams on the brakes. After putting the car in park, he reaches for Tali's hand. She pulls it away. He moves closer to her. She stares out the passenger window as tears stream down her face. He starts to speak and then changes his mind. Instead, he refastens his seat belt and starts driving. After a few minutes pass, he says, "Would you like some coffee when we get home?"

No response. The remainder of the drive is made in silence. Blake pulls the car into the garage. Tali gets out of the car and goes inside, closing the door behind her. Jasper jumps up to greet Tali with tail wagging and happy barks. Tali kneels on the floor to hug Jasper and look into her peaceful brown eyes. For a moment, Tali wishes she and Jasper and Misty could just leave and never look back. Misty pads over to Tali and paws at her. Tali picks up Misty and holds her close.

She hears Blake's footsteps as Jasper runs to him. "How's my lady?" he asks as he bends down to pet her. "Tali, Jasper sure has a lot of energy tonight! I'll take her on a short walk to calm her down a little. Want to go with us?"

"No, thanks," says Tali.

As Blake grabs the leash and heads out the front door, Tali sinks onto the floor in a puddle of tears. 'Why? What's going on in Blake's head? Why does he yell at me and criticize me all the time? Maybe he's going through something at work and takes his anger out on me. That's probably it. He'll be better after walking Jasper and a good night's sleep. Yeah, tomorrow will be better,' she tells herself. She realizes that he will be coming through the door with Jasper soon, and he always gets mad at her when she cries, so she stands up and goes into the powder room to dry her eyes and fix her makeup before he gets back.

Tali is flipping through cookbook pages with Misty sitting beside her when Blake gets home with the dog. "Hey!" he says. "Whatcha doing?"

She replies, "I'm looking for some new recipes for the cookout here next weekend. Thinking the theme will be Mediterranean this time."

"Okay, sounds good. I haven't gotten any yes RSVPs at work yet, only nos. Still waiting to hear about seven more invitations. How about you?"

She replies, "All of my friends and colleagues except for two have responded with yes. Looks like we have forty-nine people coming so far, and then I'll add any responses from your work list. Should be a fun gathering."

"Wow, Tali! I don't have friends like you do." Tali remains silent. She has listened to Blake complain about people not liking him and not having friends the whole time they've been together. Earlier this year before Blake started his new job, they even paid out of their own pocket for him to attend training programs, but it didn't change anything. He still has no friends. He has asked her for advice, and she's shared insights and suggestions for helping him get to know people and build relationships. Each time, he acts like he appreciates her advice, and then he continues to try to micromanage people in his life by being controlling and manipulative. He continually pisses people off...including his wife. Tonight has been difficult—typical yet difficult. Something needs to change, and soon.

Tali sneaks off to the stairs and climbs the circular staircase to the master bedroom in their Georgian-style townhouse. She is fatigued from Blake's rage session and subsequent politeness. He's so chaotic. She never knows which way the wind is blowing and where his emotions are going to land when they're together. She is questioning, again, why she fell in love with him in the first place. She's been researching personality disorders to try to figure out what's going on with Blake. What drew her to him?

Tali opens her laptop to study her notes from her sessions with Shannon. Then she opens the book *Stop Walking on Eggshells* by Paul T. Mason, MS and Randi Kreger and begins to read.

38

Depression

Sunday afternoon after the dinner party, Tali and Blake are sitting on the terrace working on their computers. Tali's working on design ideas for a new client while Blake's responding to an email from a potential new employer in Monterey. They want to interview him on Wednesday of this coming week. He begins a conversation with Tali about the new job opportunity. Later that day, Blake is depressed and confides in Tali that he's having suicidal thoughts. On Monday, he stays home from work. Tali calls Sydney, tells her about Blake, and let's her know she'll be working from home.

On Tuesday, Tali takes the day off and drives with Blake to his interview in Monterey. The interview goes well on Wednesday. They drive back to Newport Beach after the interview. They both go back to work on Thursday. The rest of the week and the weekend go by uneventfully. Then Blake gets a call on Monday with an offer for the job in Monterey. He and Tali talk over dinner. He accepts the job offer.

He gives his current employer two weeks' notice. Tali helps Blake pack up his cubicle at work and suitcases at home. His new company has a corporate apartment for him to live in until he gets settled into the area and he and Tali look for a new place. Blake is thinking about how to approach the subject of finding a new job for her in Monterey.

39

Once a Rager, Always a Rager

Friday evening before Blake leaves for Monterey, Tali hosts a casual dinner with friends to congratulate Blake and wish him success in his new job. She cooks Blake's favorite foods. Throughout the evening, Blake and others were complimenting Tali on the wonderful meal she prepared, and he was talking about how he loves the new decor she's putting into her art studio/office upstairs. He even took people up to the room to show them her work. Everyone hugged Blake and congratulated him throughout the evening. Blake seemed to enjoy the evening.

As the evening concludes, the last few guests depart with hugs and well wishes for Blake's new job opportunity in Monterey. Blake smiles as he closes the front door, but then he turns toward Tali with a look of contempt in his eyes. He's waited for everyone to leave to blast Tali and tear her down.

She looks at him and says, "What's wrong? You look upset."

"Everyone here tonight really seems to like you better than me. I felt their loathing all night, Tali."

"That's ridiculous, babe," she says. "They came here to celebrate you. Don't turn this lovely gathering with friends into a negative experience centered on you!"

He says, "What do you mean by that comment?"

After a deep breath, she simply looks at him and says, "I'm gonna clean up here, and then I'm going upstairs. I have a few calls to make."

"Oh, you're probably gonna call Molly and Bentley to complain about me."

Tali looks at him with pity in her eyes and says, "I just have a few calls to make." She turns into the dining room to begin clearing the table and extinguishing the candles. Blake goes to the family room to sit on his end of the leather couch, opens his laptop, and turns on the TV. Tali finishes cleaning the dining room and kitchen and stores the leftovers. Silently, she ascends the stairs with Jasper and Misty following close behind her. They go into her art room and settle on the chaise. She texts Molly and Bentley, her thoughts chaotic.

40

Will the Mask Stay On?

Blake leaves Saturday morning and begins to settle into Monterey over the weekend. When he arrives at his new office on Monday morning, his boss and coworkers greet him and give him a tour of the floor. His office window overlooks a local artisan market. He thinks, 'Tali would like this location.'

It doesn't take his coworkers long to realize that he thinks he's the smartest person in the room. He starts irritating coworkers within the first two weeks. At first, they think he's just nervous, but then they realize that he's a jerk.

Tali's friends come over to her townhouse Sunday evening after Blake leaves. They order pizza and just hang out and talk.

Three weeks later, Blake arrives at the Ocean Grill in Monterey to meet a potential new client who is considering hiring his firm as her financial advisory team. This potential client, Jessica Tori, is CEO of Blaze, Inc., and is known for her hard-hitting personality. Blake met Jessica while running on the beach last weekend. He's been doing some research. Jessica's company has grown from $10 million to $150 billion in assets within the last seven years through leadership in innovation and biotech patents. The company is headquartered in Silicon Valley, and Jessica is seeking new ideas for managing short-term liquidity for pilot studies and long-term asset management for capital innovation projects. He thinks he's convinced her to hire him as her new financial advisor. Her previous advisor just went to prison for insider trading on her company. Blake believes one exquisite dinner meeting with him will convince her to hire his firm. He knows that such a coup would shine a light on him in the eyes of his boss and colleagues. 'Then they'll know that I'm the smartest, best hire ever,' he thinks as he marches up to the maître d' at 6:45 p.m. and says he has a reservation for two at 7:00 p.m. The maître d' informs him that his dinner companion has already arrived and leads Blake to their table by the window with a spectacular sunset view.

"Hi, Jessica," Blake says as he reaches to shake her hand. She stands and smiles as she accepts his handshake.

She says, "Yes, nice to see you again." They exchange small talk as she retakes her seat and Blake sits across from her. During dinner, they discuss Blake's ideas for asset management for her growing company. She listens, but ultimately, she is not impressed with his pompous attitude and unorthodox methods that he's proposing for a long-term business growth strategy, especially with the current potential onslaught of an influenza pandemic that will potentially affect supply chain management streams and all global financial markets. She is a very bright woman and makes it quite clear that she doesn't buy into Blake's schemes.

It was a tough evening and meeting, so Blake stays after Jessica leaves. He sits at the bar for a while, finally leaving around eleven. He calls Tali on his way home to rant about his new job, his coworkers, and the difficult dinner meeting he just had. She listens while sitting at her office drafting table looking over the designs she must present on Monday morning. When he finishes his raging monologue, Tali says, "Oh no, Blake. I'm sorry you're having a bad day. How can I help you?"

"You can come visit next weekend," he says. "How about it? I can show you around the city. We need some time together to reconnect, Tali."

She says, "Okay. My three projects all go to Sydney this coming week for review. This is good timing. Sure. I'll drive up after work on Friday."

Blake says, "That's great! I can't wait to see you. I've missed you so much."

Tali replies, "Me too."

Dear Josie… Blake seems to be wearing a "virtual mask" where he sometimes shows people outside of our marital relationship a different personality… Reminds me of the iceberg analogy where we see the ice above the waterline, when reality there is dramatically more ice below the surface of the water. Blake's trying to hide what's below the surface… his evil side.

41

Impact

Tali Solace loses herself in thought as she drives her metallic blue Mustang convertible on the PCH from L.A. to Monterey. The sun is setting over the waves crashing into the shore to her left. She glances at the digital clock in the dash. Still four more hours of driving to get to their friend's new condo on Del Monte Beach in Monterey where she will meet up with Blake. The two of them are staying for the weekend while they look at houses in the area. She's not really sure why she's making this trip tonight. Tali completed the three design projects this week that she had mentioned to Blake. Work has been going well, and with her recent pay raise, she decided to lease a blue Mustang convertible. A friend at the dealership helped her negotiate the deal. Blake has been inviting her to come every weekend for the past month, ever since he took the new job or, as he calls it, "the promotion I've been waiting for." Tali has been busy with work since Blake relocated to Monterey. Ever since they married nearly three years ago on Grace Beach, they have spent a lot of time together, until this job.

It is now July, and she has been avoiding this drive to see him. She's not sure why. It's easier to not think about it, or him…or their marriage. Blake likes to be in control, and she isn't sure this move is in her best interest, but Blake persuaded her to agree to it after he quit his job in Newport Beach. To this day, she still wonders why he quit. He never gave her a straight, plausible answer. She heard rumors of a possible sexual harassment charge against him, but she never learned the details. She has her own work to focus on, and Sydney has been hinting that there have been some recent potential partnership conversations between the partners in the interior design firm where she has been working since she graduated from college. Last week, the firm won the contract bid for designing the lobby and meeting rooms for the upcoming renovations of the Newport Beach Convention Center. She doesn't have time to move right now…and doesn't really want to. She turns up the volume on her playlist and tries to drown out her own thoughts of doubt and dread. On the positive side, traffic is flowing pretty smoothly up the PCH for a Friday evening.

She drives another hour and then pulls off the highway at a gas station. She stops the car and goes into the convenience store to buy a bottle of water and some gum. When she gets back into the car, she checks her messages. Blake texted her to see how her trip was going. She quickly texts back with her ETA. He replies with "B safe. C U soon. Xoxo"

She starts the car, buckles her seatbelt, pushes "resume" on her GPS, and gets back onto the highway headed toward Monterey. Two hours later, she is about an hour away from their friends' place. She notices that the traffic has thinned out dramatically. She thinks it's kind of strange to not see any cars on her side of the highway. Then, off in the distance ahead of her, she sees some flashing blue lights. She checks her speedometer, making sure she's under the speed limit. As she continues driving, she thinks that she now sees flashing lights on both sides of the highway. 'Oh, great,' she sighs. 'Just what I need tonight, a drug traffic checkpoint delay.'

"Oh my, God," she cries. She turns the wheel hard to the right to swerve out of the way of an oncoming car that's driving the wrong way on her side of the highway. She hits the guardrail on the right. Her car spins out of control across the lanes and goes over the cliff toward the beach. For a few seconds, all she hears is silence.

Tali's car comes to a stop between some rocks on the coastline below the highway. She feels water all around her as she tries to open her eyes. After a few seconds, she realizes that the seatbelt is holding her to the seat and she is actually upside down. Apparently, the car has landed on its roof. She falls unconscious.

She awakens to the tender voice and touch on her neck of a man kneeling beside her vehicle's crushed driver-side window. He says, "Ma'am, I'm just checking your pulse. You're going to be okay. Help is on the way."

She can barely see whoever this person is beside her car. It's like there is a bright light shining in her face. She cannot hear anything. She feels the water moving around her. She licks her lips… The taste of blood and salt fill her mouth. She falls unconscious again.

Later, she awakens to the sound of crashing waves…muffled voices…and something else… metal scraping against metal. Tali screams, "It's too loud! Stop it! Get me out of here!"

The man beside the car touches her shoulder and says, "They're trying to get you out of the car. The tide's rising a little. I'm here with you. Keep breathing." He gently caresses her shoulder. He can see the compound fracture with the bones protruding from her lower arm and the steering column pinning what's left of her legs. He continues to talk to her as the rescuers work to free her from the vehicle. In a state of shock, she fades into unconsciousness once again.

42

Problems Compound

Forty five minutes later, she awakens as the paramedics are putting an oxygen mask on her, tourniquets on the two compound fractures to her right radius and ulna and to her right tibia and fibula, and they are working to stabilize her vitals the best they can before loading her into an air ambulance. She tries to talk in a very raspy and hauntingly broken voice, "Tell that man…who came…stayed…thanks…" She trails off as the sedative they injected into her fluid line takes effect. They finish prepping her for the helicopter ride to the hospital.

The ER docs are waiting beside the rooftop helipad when the air ambulance lands on the hospital. The paramedics unload Tali and help transfer her to a gurney. While doing so, they are filling the docs in on Tali's accident and initial treatments as the medical team rushes her to the elevator. The paramedics then tell them that there were pools of blood surrounding Tali in her automobile and, of course, about the obvious compound fractures.

The ER doctor on call, Dr. William Knowles, has recently completed his residency at a Memphis hospital and is now doing a fellowship in Trauma Orthopedics. The ER trauma resident, Dr. Thadeus Brooks, and the ER medical team wheel the gurney containing Tali into a treatment room where Dr. Knowles meets them to examine the patient, rushing to control the bleeding and trying to stabilize Tali. Her injuries include head injury, shattered right arm with compound fractures, internal bleeding, shattered pelvis, both hips broken, shattered right leg with compound fracture, broken right ankle, torn ligaments in both knees, and shattered left foot. The ER team does not expect Tali to live, but they continue working to stabilize her vitals and save her life. Her blood pressure plummets. She is still unconscious, her body in shock from the trauma. The gash on the right side of her head continues to bleed profusely.

Dr. Brooks opens Tali's abdominal cavity to search for the source(s) of the internal bleeding. Once the cavity is open, he tries to clamp, suture, and contain the bleeds, but so many organs are bleeding that he closes her up and tells the team that Tali's blood loss is irreparable. They continue the blood transfusions, and Dr. Knowles tries to reposition the remaining pieces of bones in Tali's right arm and right leg by surgically opening the limbs — not an easy task. Bone fragments are lodged into the cartilage of her joints — elbow, hips, knees, and ankles. She continues to bleed internally, and her left foot is unrecognizable. The surgeons reattach fragments of her left foot with surgical pins. And then they suspend her mangled foot in an air cast until they can get her other bleeding under control and piece her right arm and right leg back together with metal rods, plates, and screws. They also install metal plates and screws into the shattered left side of her pelvis.

43

Who Can You Call?

When the police locate Tali's emergency contacts information—Tali's Mamita, Molly, Bentley, and Sydney— they contact each person. While Tali is in emergency surgery, Blake receives a call from Sydney to inform him that Tali has been in a car accident and she is in the hospital ER. She gives him the address of the hospital. Blake packs his laptop and some clothes and then drives to the hospital. When he arrives at the hospital admissions desk, the nurse calmly informs him that Tali is still in emergency surgery.

Blake says, "I have to see my wife! Where the hell is she?"

The nurse says, "Please calm down, Mr. Solace. I will page a doctor to talk with you about your wife's condition."

Blake stares at her with rage in his eyes and then walks over to a chair in the hallway to sit down. He holds his head in his hands as he rests his elbows on his knees. Dr. Brooks, the trauma resident, approaches him. "Mr. Solace? I'm Dr. Brooks. I was here when your wife arrived in the air ambulance. Currently, Dr. Knowles, our best Trauma Orthopedic surgeon, is operating on your wife to repair two compound fractures, one on her right arm and one on her right leg. Once those injuries are contained, Dr. Knowles will analyze your wife's stability and decide the timing for the initial repairs of both sides of her right ankle, the rebuild of her left foot, and reconstruction of her crushed pelvis and each of her broken hips. She is still bleeding internally. It has subsided a bit. We are monitoring and infusing as needed." Dr. Brooks waits patiently for Blake to process the difficult news.

Blake sits silently for a few minutes, staring at his hands while he contemplates this situation. 'Wow,' he thinks. 'This is bad. This is really bad.'

"What is her prognosis?" Blake finally asks Dr. Brooks.

"She's in very critical condition, Mr. Solace. We are doing everything we can to save her, but to be honest, it doesn't look good. I'm sorry, Mr. Solace."

Blake doesn't know what to say. He thinks, 'This messes up mine and Tali's weekend plans. I was going to wine and dine her and convince her to leave her job in Newport Beach and move to Monterey to be with me.' He whispers, "May I see her?"

Dr. Brooks replies, "She's still in surgery with Dr. Knowles. He'll come speak with you when Tali's out of surgery."

44

Prognosis

Four hours later, at four in the morning, Dr. Knowles enters the surgical waiting room. Blake and one woman are the only two people in the waiting area. Dr. Knowles approaches Blake and sits down in the chair beside him. He has a very concerned expression on his face. "Mr. Solace," he begins, "your wife has survived the repairs of her two compound fractures, the implantation of metal rods, plates, screws, and a metal plate in an attempt to stabilize her crushed pelvis. We've also done a reconstruction of her right ankle. If she awakens within the next five days and her vitals are stable, we will rebuild her left foot. Both of Tali's hips were shattered. The internal bleeding seems to have halted for now, which is very good news. We will continue to monitor her. If she awakens, she'll be non-weight-bearing for a while until we see sufficient progress in the healing of the skeletal fractures—in particular, her right leg and ankle, her left foot, and the pelvis and hip joints. Mr. Solace, we do not expect a full recovery. I'm sorry. Tali will probably never walk again nor ever regain full use of her right arm again. The injuries were too severe. We did and will continue to do our best. Only time will tell."

Blake just sits there with his head in his hands staring at the floor. He has no words. Finally, he says, "When may I see her?"

"She's being transferred to the Trauma ICU right now. You can see her for ten minutes if you would like. She's still sedated from the surgical anesthesia."

"Yes, please take me to her," Blake says. Dr. Knowles leads Blake through the locked doors of the Trauma ICU and over to Tali's bedside. Blake stands there beside her bed. He's quiet. She is barely recognizable with all the bandages and the swelling from her body being in shock. He reaches to touch her left hand, the only portion of her that's not covered in bandages. After ten minutes have passed, the nurse comes over to tell him that it's time to go. She tells him that he may come back in an hour for another ten-minute visit. He thanks her and says he'll be back in an hour. He goes back to the waiting area to get some coffee. Then he goes out to his car to get his laptop bag.

*****

After nine days of being in a coma, on a ventilator, while in the Trauma ICU, and having endured five of the ten surgeries required to rebuild her broken body, Tali tries to open her eyes. A nurse notices and reaches for Tali's left shoulder, trying to reassure her that she is okay. Tali, her expression frantic, tries to move her head and her left arm (the only limb that is not completely bandaged and immobilized).

45

The Daily Journey

After four weeks in the hospital, Tali is admitted to an orthopedic rehabilitation hospital in Newport Beach to begin physical therapy and determine what functions she can recover. Her doctors are skeptical that she will ever regain the use of her legs or right arm, as so much trauma occurred to those three limbs.

Tali can see her right arm and both legs, but she cannot make those three limbs move. She learns to move about in a wheelchair with a lever on the left side that she uses with her left hand to propel and steer the wheelchair. Since she is right-handed, Tali wonders, 'Will I ever draw or paint again?' Depression begins to set into her psyche.

Sydney, Molly, Bentley, Tali's friends from work, neighbors, her trainer Ryan, high school friends, and her parents all pitch in to be a supportive team to help Tali heal. They encourage her daily. Tali's so thankful for her family and friends.

Blake pays more attention to his work in Monterey than he does to Tali. He says that he needs to work hard to keep his new job. Sydney overheard Blake on the phone with someone who was asking him to referee a pee-wee soccer game this week, which he agreed to do.

46

Life = 10% What Happens + 90% What You Do About It

Tali is concerned about her lack of progress with her work at the interior design firm. Sydney oversees adaptations to Tali's office for wheelchair accessibility (adjustable drafting table, adjustable desk, open areas wide enough for navigating a wheelchair in the office space) so that when Tali is released from the rehabilitation hospital, she will be as comfortable as possible. Sydney tells her that there's no pressure to come back to work until she's ready. Tali is working with the occupational therapist at the rehab hospital learning how to transfer to and from the wheelchair using a sliding board and how to retrieve objects with a tool called a reacher.

She tells the OT, "This will be perfect for picking up Jasper's and Misty's toys off the floor." Ryan's role is to help her with the routines that her physical therapist prescribes for her. She's gradually regaining some movement in her right arm, but learning how to work with implanted metal joints is challenging. Grasping objects is still difficult. She continues to try, hoping to hold a pencil and paintbrush again one day.

47

Good Samaritan...Angel

Eight weeks after the car wreck, a California Highway Patrol officer who was on duty the night of the accident calls Tali to tell her the story of what happened.

He says, "We set up roadblocks because there was a wrong-way driver on PCH that night who had evaded our pursuit for thirty miles. When your headlights came into view, it appeared that the other driver was was headed straight for you, driving head-on in your lane. You swerved out of her way, but then you hit the guardrail, and that impact sent your car spinning toward the other lane and then you went over the cliff.

"Tali, you mentioned a man who found your car and stayed with you? No one called 911 about your car. No other people were on the beach there that night when our police rescue team arrived to extract you from the vehicle. I saw you go over the cliff because I was pursuing the wrong-way driver who was trying to hit you. Did this man you mentioned say anything to you?"

She is silent for a few seconds as she tries to remember. She replies, "I'm not sure. I think he told me to breathe. I'm not sure what else he said. I just remember feeling glad that he was there with me, and I would like to thank him. Do you know where he is?"

Dear Josie… Are angels real? I think that man who stayed with me after the wreck could have been an angel… No one else seems to have seen him…

48

One Day at a Time

Blake comes back to Newport Beach for a few weeks when Tali begins physical therapy at the rehabilitation hospital. He convinces his new boss in Monterey that he can continue to work remotely and that he should be there to help Tali get settled back into their (her) home while she figures out how to go back to work. The trouble is, Blake continues to ignore Tali pretty much except for occasional visits to her room at the rehab hospital to review her chart and progress.

Molly recalls that while Tali was still having emergency surgeries with the possibility of dying on the table or from complications, Blake told her, "No, you cannot have my cell phone number. You might give it to someone." Molly then talked with Bentley, who had Blake's number since Blake would call him to convince him that there was something wrong with Tali's behaviors. Molly decides not to mention this peculiar incident to Tali. She already has enough on her mind.

49

New Direction

Tali has new ideas for her interior designs going forward. Her passion is now to make interior designs accessible for people in wheelchairs or getting around with other gait aids. She reaches out to Sami, her architect friend, to collaborate on design ideas. The community development consultant wants to talk with Tali about this topic. The Newport Beach Convention Center client has been on hold waiting for Tali to heal and get out of the hospital to continue planning the remodel. They are excited to talk with Tali about her new insights into accessibility. Tali and Sydney eagerly discuss ideas and clients.

Dear Josie… I'm still trying to recover from the wreck. The pain…every day…I don't talk about it, but I know others notice. I'm trying to heal. This is so hard. My orthopedic surgeon says that hopefully I will be weight-bearing enough to try to learn to walk again in a few weeks. I hope so. In the meantime, I'm working on some designs for accessibility in public buildings. Living in a wheelchair for a few months has taught me that we need to be more attentive to accessibility for people in wheelchairs and those who use other gait aids. I'm learning so much and trying to do something positive while I work to heal from this trauma.

A few days later, Tali has been declared fit for weight-bearing after her X-rays indicate enough healing has occurred. She beings working with her physical therapist and Ryan to learn how to use a walker. A couple weeks later, Molly drives her to work and helps her ambulate into the interior design firm with her walker. Everyone claps and cheers for Tali.

50

Do You Believe in Miracles?

Twelve months after the car wreck, Tali and Blake are strolling on the beach in Newport Beach at sunset. Tali says, "You know…the docs said I'd never be doing this again. Miracles do happen." She looks over at Blake as she awaits his comment.

"Yeah…guess the docs were wrong about you, Tali. You've always done what you say you're gonna do. You told them that you were gonna walk again! Look at you, babe! You are! It's been tough though, right?"

"Yeah…really hard. The pain. The setbacks. I'm thankful for everyone in my life who's been there for me to help me recover. It's been a journey."

They walk along the shore in silence. Blake asks, "What does your future look like, Tali? Are you going to move to Monterey to be with me? Do you want to have a family with me? Or are you even able to conceive a child after all your body has endured?"

She replies, "Blake, do you think you're going to make this job work?"

Blake replies, "Yes, babe! I think this one's The One. Come be with me."

"Okay," Tali says. "I'll discuss this idea further with Sydney."

Blake turns to face Tali. He kisses her very passionately and then whispers, "Thank you. You won't regret this move. I promise."

Tali recognizes how carefully she is avoiding telling Blake she's not going to move.

51

Gaslighting

During the next few days, Tali receives multiple calls from her friends whom Blake has contacted trying to convince them that Tali has brain damage from the car wreck. Blake calls Tali's Mamita to talk about Tali's progress since the wreck. "I'm concerned about Tali's mental state."

Mamita assures Blake that Tali has recovered from the wreck, and she is as sharp as ever. She adds, "Blake, you better watch out. Tali's been through hell, and now she's a survivor. She has a new lease on life, and she's not going to waste this second chance to achieve her goals. She's thinking circles around everyone these days!"

Blake replies with, "Um…yeah, sure, whatever you say. She'll never be better than me… She's just the brawn and I'm the brains of this marital duo."

Mamita rolls her eyes. After they hang up, she texts Tali, "Are you busy?"

52

Washing Away the F.E.A.R.

Tali and her Mamita decide to spend a few days together in San Diego. They stay at a quaint inn on the beach. Early in the morning, Tali takes the boardwalk to the beach. As the sun is rising in the east, she sees a few beach walkers bending down to pick up shiny shells washed onto shore by the night tides. A jogger greets her with a cheerful, "Good morning!" as she steps into the sand.

She replies, "Good morning!" She approaches the two men setting up chairs and umbrellas for daily rental. She selects two chairs and pays them the rental fee. She brought two beach towels with her to drape over each chair to stake their claim until she and her Mamita come down to the beach after breakfast. Tali strolls along the shore as she witnesses the sun rising and the seagulls seeking out their marine fare on this new day. She's thinking and wondering as she walks, 'Why am I so unhappy? I have a great job. Many friends. A nice home. I'm so thankful to be at the beach, to be able to think without Blake's condescending attitude and judgment clouding my thoughts.' Tali stops for a moment, faces the waves, and stares out into the massive ocean. Water spans as far as the eyes can see. On the horizon, there's not a cloud in the sky. She closes her eyes and listens intently to the sounds of the surf and the birds. She opens her eyes and continues her stroll along the shoreline. Whatever is going on in her life right now feels overwhelming, but being here at the beach is helping put her difficulties into a bubble…or a box… like compartmentalizing the situation so that she can more effectively identify what's going on with Blake and then figure out a solution so that his bizarre behaviors will not continue to permeate her every moment and thoughts as they have been.

Tali is currently struggling with her memory, confidence, and attention to detail in her work projects. Sydney and her co-workers have been supportive, but she doesn't want to push the envelope on how long they will "put up" with her lack of productivity. 'Where is the resilience that I used to have? Persistence? Perseverance? And I've lost my sense of humor. What is wrong with me?' She stops again to ask herself the hard question. 'What am I afraid of? Has Blake made me fearful?' She stares at the waves, thinking about times in her life when situations felt overwhelming and how she handled those times. Since she married Blake, she has drifted away from old friends with whom she used to talk about life stuff. Occasionally, those friends would drag her to a retreat, somewhere out in nature with lakes and waterfalls, to help her recognize the spiritual side of life and that God will help her with any problem she's facing. Tali turns around to head back up the beach to the inn to meet up with her Mamita for breakfast. She feels a little better.

She wants to talk with her about Blake and the idea that he is exhibiting a narcissistic personality disorder.

Tali shares her thoughts and her fear of Blake. It's been thirteen months since the car wreck. Tali has so many thoughts racing through her mind. She feels blessed to have this quiet time with her Mamita. After a few days, the two ladies return to their own realities. The long walks on the beach were therapeutic in multiple ways. Tali's gait continues to improve. While at the inn, she noticed a need for accessibility for people who are in wheelchairs or needing to use gait aids for mobility. She texts Sydney with some ideas to discuss when she returns to the office tomorrow.

53

Exposure

Blake catches the new strain of influenza that is currently circulating the globe. Deaths in certain locations have been reported. Everyone is advised to use extreme caution and wear a mask when in public to try to contain the virus and prevent spreading. He had been playing pool a few days earlier with someone who he learns has the new flu strain, but Blake refuses to get tested.

Blake goes to a baseball game to meet a potential client in San Francisco while he is feeling ill. He mingles with the potential client and other guests in their corporate box seats at the baseball stadium.

The next day he shows up at work, still ill. His coworkers threaten to contact corporate legal counsel on him if doesn't get tested. Blake's boss steps in and makes him go get tested. He calls the office on his way home and says he probably has allergies. "The doc gave me a decongestant."

The next day when his test comes back positive, he again calls his boss, who tells him the potential client he met at the baseball game has caught the flu from Blake. That ends that potential future client relationship.

He does not tell Tali about what happened. He just acts like he's extremely busy with work during his recovery quarantine week. He thinks since he lost the client that she might doubt his longevity at the Monterey firm and not move to Monterey. He doesn't want to cause any doubts. He must have her there with him.

54

He Has No Friends

When Blake visits Newport Beach, he only wants to have dinner and spend time with Tali. She wants them to hang out with her friend and her friend's husband. At this point, Tali is afraid to always be alone with him. Blake refuses. "I just want to be alone with you. Besides, your friends hate me."

Blake continues to complain that no one at his work likes him. He says he has more experience and that he's the smartest person at his work. Tali is starting to think that he's not telling her the truth about his job.

55

Noise at 4:00 a.m. to No More Lint

While still at their Newport Beach townhome, Blake empties the dishwasher, loudly putting away the dishes at four in the morning. He grabs stacks of plates out of the dishwasher, and the plates collide as he noisily stacks them onto the shelf and slams the cabinet door. Tali makes a mental note to have the contractor install soft-close drawers and cabinet doors when she decides to remodel the kitchen. She's thinking about staying in Newport Beach awhile longer. Tali quietly enters the room where Blake is busily slamming drawers and cabinet doors. He has jazz trumpet music playing in the background. He announces, "I couldn't sleep, so I thought I'd get a jump on these chores since you never seem to have time to do the dishes."

Then he disappears into the laundry room. He pulls a load of clothes out of the dryer and places a load from the washer into the dryer. He carries the basket of dry clothes into the family room where Tali is sitting with a cup of coffee. Blake begins to inspect the laundry and then suddenly goes into a rage.

"I'm so tired of clothes being left in the dryer after they're dried and then they get wrinkled and have to be washed and dried all over again to get the wrinkles out. And look at my socks!" he shouts. "They always have lint on them. Don't you know how to do laundry, Tali? You're no good. I thought I told you to never touch my laundry again. Never."

Tali just sits there quietly. Then she stands up and walks to the terrace door, grabbing a hoodie off the chair. On the terrace, she notes it isn't yet five. She sits down on the chaise as the sky illuminates with the impending sunrise. When her eyes well up with tears, she fights the urge to cry, but she can't help it. She opens her notes app on her smartphone and writes.

Dear Josie… I need help… I just cannot understand why Blake is so bitter and judgmental. He criticizes everything I do. Is it me? He says I'm to blame for our marital problems. Maybe he's right.

After sunrise, when Tali comes back inside, she hears Blake talking on the phone with his older brother about his new laundry methods. He says he has figured out the best ways to do laundry, and he bought this great new detergent in Monterey. It's 6 a.m., and he's pontificating about the best ways to do laundry.

Tali passes him silently and goes into the master bedroom to get ready for the day. What a strange and twisted start to Monday morning. Maybe working at the office today will help take her mind off of Blake's absurd outrage about laundry. His rages are becoming a daily occurrence. Tali never knows what his mood will be when she walks through the door in the evenings.

He's still working remotely. She wonders when he's going back to Monterey.

She has been keeping a log of his behaviors and is starting to see a pattern. He seems to be deliberately adding chaos to situations when he doesn't feel like he is in control. It's as if he always has to be in control and tear down other people to make himself feel more grand.

56

From Then to Now

ack in Monterey, Blake pauses before leaving his office to follow up with his boss, Cam, regarding the rejected project. He knows his boss will grill him in their meeting this morning regarding next steps to adjust the analysis for the new product to get it approved by the risk committee. Blake's plan is to take all the emails from his team explaining why it is their fault (and not his) the project was rejected. He demanded that each employee on his team craft an email of how they were responsible for the project failure to remove the blame from Blake. He has reviewed each one and feels like they make a good case.

He knows that he needs to be careful. He knows that over the past several years, he has job-hopped for various reasons, including being fired. This position is one of the few in the country that matched his skill set and gave him an opportunity for growth and promotion. It has the possibility of even taking him into age-related retirement with benefits like being tenured for a pension, a rare offering these days.

Blake tends to be responsive to "tough love" authority due to the household environment fostered by his controlling, dominating, and manipulative mother. She controls everyone in Blake's family—his father, his older brother, and himself. Blake realizes that he's becoming like her. He's proud of himself. Growing up, he was still very strong-willed. He felt he was always right and never wrong no matter what anyone else said or did in a particular situation. He believes he is intellectually superior to everyone else in the company and feels he is undercompensated and underappreciated for what he contributes to the company.

Before going to meet with his boss, Blake subconsciously puts on an invisible mask. Its purpose is to try to hide, if necessary, any actual visible reaction he might have to anything his boss says that could reflect negatively on Blake. He doesn't want a mandated direction of next steps that he doesn't agree with. He also does a routine check using the full-length mirror he had mounted on the back of his office door to be sure every hair is in place, his white button-down shirt collar and red tie are not awry, and his navy blazer and freshly creased dark gray wool trousers look their best. He steamed them this morning since he banned Tali from ever touching his laundry again. And, of course, his shoes are shined. He decided to dress up a bit rather than wear a green polo with the company logo and khakis. As he tugs on the Windsor knot of his tie, he practices his courtesy smile and listens to his perfunctory "heh-heh" laugh that he occasionally volunteers in conversations, even when he doesn't think someone's witty comment deserves an acknowledgment or any response from him. Humility as a rule is not in his vocabulary, but it is part of the mask.

When Blake enters his boss's office at the agreed-upon time, he speaks first by saying, "Good morning."

His boss replies, "Have a seat," and motions him to sit down in one of the two chairs in front of his desk.

Blake takes this as a sign that this will be a power meeting. Sitting in the chair has his boss talking down to him as opposed to a more level playing field when sitting at the small round conference table in the corner of his office. He immediately and inappropriately jumps in by saying, "I met yesterday afternoon with my team, who had direct involvement in the assessment of the project that was rejected by the risk committee. I asked each of them to submit their comments to me before they left the office yesterday in an email outlining their role in the project and how they could have performed their task differently to avoid what happened. They each have offered their apologies. Here are copies for you. I highlighted the key points made by each individual."

Cam responds, "Blake, that is fine, but don't you think there is a key piece of the puzzle missing? What was your role in this less-than-satisfactory outcome, and what are your plans to be a true leader and get this back on track?"

As a rule, Blake doesn't think fast on his feet. He has not prepped himself to be able to respond to Cam's question and is totally taken off guard. He responds, "Sir, I do have some recommendations and would like to get back on your calendar tomorrow afternoon to discuss them with you in detail." Blake is lying, knowing he currently has no ideas. But he knows he could come up with something in twenty-four hours by getting his team back together in think-tank mode.

He walks dejectedly back to his office, thinking, 'I need more time to process this situation.' He feels his mask melting with every step as his inner rage is growing. He slithers to his car, avoiding any contact with anyone, and takes an early lunch by himself to try to recover.

Meanwhile, Cam returns a call to the head of Human Resources. The discussion is to have lunch sometime this week to catch up on Blake. One of Blake's team had complained about his rant yesterday to HR. After he hangs up, Cam acknowledges to himself that Blake is technically one of the smartest in the company, but he asks himself silently, 'Is he one of the best from a maturity and leadership standpoint?'

Blake feels tired as he climbs into his SUV right at five o'clock to drive home to his condominium. He's thinking Chinese delivery for dinner. He wishes Tali would be there so he could tell her all about his awful day. He dials her number.

She answers, "Hi, Blake! What's new? How's your day?"

He replies, "It's been a rough day at work and has taken a major emotional toll on me. I wish you were here. This morning I got a call that an analysis and recommendation for a new product that my team prepared had been submitted to the risk committee for review and approval, but it got rejected. Cam wasn't impressed and spoke very sternly to me, blaming me for not managing my team to avoid this happening. I tried to respond with answers from my employees admitting the blame for the project failure, but Cam didn't buy it. He expected me to share in the blame! Seriously? Why would it be my fault? My employees are the losers that made the mistakes. I told Cam I would follow up with my team and meet with him tomorrow afternoon." Blake is screaming at this point in the monologue about his day. "Tali, what should I do? Everyone hates me here."

Tali is silent for a few seconds and then replies, "Oh dear, I'm not sure what to say, Blake." She pauses and then adds, "Do you think you should have reviewed your team's work in more detail? You said that there were mistakes in the calculations and that's why the risk committee rejected the project?"

Blake screams, "Those idiots need to take responsibility for their own work! It's not my job to hold their hands, Tali! This is not my fault!"

Tali says, "Blake, don't yell at me. I'm going to let you go and calm down. I'll text you later to see if you would like to talk more calmly about this. I love you." She ends the call.

Blake mutters something under his breath and then he asks Siri to call the Chinese restaurant so that he can order dinner to be delivered when he gets home.

After dinner and a few beers, Blake decides to go back to his office. He closes the door and stares out his window noticing the distant interstate full of slow-moving traffic going east. "Must be a wreck," Blake mutters to himself while thinking this is not the only wreck he was aware of today. He sits down at his desk and logs onto his computer to try to figure out what tale he's going to spin to convince Cam tomorrow that this failed project is not his fault.

His boss reprimanding him causes Blake to flash back to his childhood. His ears were ringing with the sound of his mother's shrieking voice, the voice she used to manage Blake when his achievements in school or life in general did not meet her higher than high expectations. The expressions of anger in his mother's voice frequently included a subset of a half-dozen phrases ad nauseam from the time Blake could remember. Alone in his office, his mind flashes back…remembering…

"It's your fault that I'm not happy."

"I've done everything for you and you're so ungrateful."

"Your poor performance is an embarrassment to the family."

"Why can't you be as good as your brother?"

"You will perform at your best to make me proud, and I define what 'your best' is."

"You're not a good son unless you measure up to my expectations."

As Blake got older, his mother manipulated him more directly with the additional phrase, "If you don't pursue the college major I chose for you, I will cut off my support."

Blake reminisces about struggling to meet all his mother's expectations. He was coerced to strive to get a doctorate in mathematics. But he failed his mother's mandate in the end as he could not handle the stress of "publish or perish" regarding research papers. At one point, he threatened his mother that he was going to commit suicide. It forced his mother's hand to back off with her academic demands but not all the others. Blake switched his major to business with a minor in music. He got his MBA on the heels of getting his undergraduate degree, then an initial job in financial analysis in manufacturing. His saga of changing jobs every few years began.

57

Mask Continues to Slip

At the office the following morning, Blake sits at his desk again thinking about his mother's tantrums. He snaps out of his frightful recollections and sends a quick email mandating all individuals who worked on the rejected project gather in the conference room next door to his office.

He slams the door and begins to rant, "I am incensed at each of you for the lack of quality on the project that was submitted yesterday morning to the risk management committee. The project was rejected, and I was singled out by my boss as being the reason it was rejected." He raised his voice even higher. "I am *not* the reason it did not pass inspection. Each of you are the reason it did not get a passing grade. I refuse to take the blame for this because it was not my fault. You each had a part in this, and each of you are the problem. I told each of you to write me an email apologizing for what you did wrong, citing how you could've done your part better. I also expected each of them to include an apology to me personally and indicating that it was not my fault. I expected to receive your emails by no later than lunchtime yesterday so that when I follow up with my boss this afternoon, I would have these in hand to review with him. Those of you who sent me emails so far…subpar…not what I asked for… No surprise there. I expect emails from every one of you by noon today. Do you understand your assignment?" The employees quickly and quietly slink out of the conference room.

Blake goes back to his office and continues to have flashbacks about growing up. He recalls his own mother's similar rants calling out his imperfections. It was always confusing to Blake that while his mother told him he was worthless, all his teachers from kindergarten throughout his school years told him he was so smart and that he had a wonderful mind. He tested as gifted and took almost every advanced class offered through high school. But he could never scholastically measure up to his mother's standards. He often felt as though he was two different people: a misfit, withdrawn child with no friends and a misfit, insecure grown man with no friends who wears a mask to try to hide the imperfections in his personality. He often feels like he would morph back and forth between the two identities, depending on the circumstances. His mom once told him the meaning of his name, Blake: dark/black or white/pale—a mysterious, dichotomous meaning.

58

Are You Busy?

The following Thursday, Blake texts Tali, "I'm driving home this weekend to be with you. If you made any plans with friends, cancel them so that you can be with me. I need to talk with you."

Tali replies, "I'm hosting dinner here Saturday evening. I'm keeping those plans with Wren, Jess, Molly, and Chad. You're welcome to hang out with us. Other than that, it's just me here with Jasper and Misty. Come on down, xoxo."

He replies, "Okay. If you won't cancel, that's fine. I'll be there tomorrow evening and drive back to Monterey on Sunday afternoon. That will give us time to be together just the two of us... with Jasper and Misty, too :)"

"Sounds good," Tali texts. "See you tomorrow."

The text, "Are you busy?" appears on Mamita's phone at 10:34 Saturday night. Tali's Mamita has learned over the past few months that when she sees that specific text from Tali, and especially at that hour of the evening, it merits a response ASAP. So, she quickly texts back a thumbs-up emoji. Within seconds, Tali's name appears on Mamita's cell phone screen. She presses the green button and says, "What's up, my dear?"

Tali responds, "I was cleaning up the kitchen after dinner tonight with friends, and I accidentally spilled the leftover green beans. Instantly, Blake went into a rant that quickly escalated. I was the victim of one of Blake's all-time rages. It was a 10-plus on a scale out of 10, with 10 being the absolute worst. Molly was there. She just now texted me to see if I'm okay. I texted her back that Blake's cooled off now. He said he had a bad week at work. I'm outside standing in the cold trying to see if Blake is wandering the townhouse looking for me. I think he's asleep. Brrr, it feels like it's below freezing with the windchill… Who knew Newport Beach could get cold temps? Probably just my feelings of shock over the evening. I'm glad I grabbed my fleece jacket on the way out of the townhouse."

She continued, "It's hard to describe. His face was redder than the reddest tomato that dad ever grew in his garden. His normally bluish eyes turned black. You couldn't tell where his pupils started and his irises ended. His voice was primal, with many words guttural and unintelligible. He repeatedly told me to shut up and that I had no right to draw a breath of air on this earth. Then in an instant, his voice and countenance would be childlike as he looked at the dog. Then he would revert to a growl with maniacal laughing as he looked back at me and my friends. Then he would go back over to Jasper and gently speak to her in a baby-talk voice about how cute she was. Then back to the rage. My friends were petrified. I quickly showed my friends to the door. After they left, he simply sat on the couch and turned on one of his favorite action movies. He fell asleep in about thirty minutes."

Tali's mom asks, "Do you know what could have triggered this, besides the green beans?"

Tali didn't have a good answer. Later that evening, she writes.

Dear Josie… I'm not sure what set off Blake after dinner this evening. I accidentally spilled the green beans while putting the bowl in the fridge. He started yelling at me in front of my friends. I called Mamita afterward to talk with her about his rages, which are becoming more intense and more frequent. Obviously, my presence irritates him.

59

More Flying Monkeys

The next morning, Tali gets a call from a former neighbor, Carrie. She suspects that Blake had confided in Carrie his thoughts about her, but she has no idea what had been said. Carrie's husband, Sam, was a buddy of Blake's, one of the few buddies Blake has ever had in his life.

Carrie asks, "How are things going, and how do you like your new townhouse? We miss having you in the neighborhood."

Tali answers cautiously, "We like it. We've met some folks that live nearby to hang out with. How are you and Sam and the children?"

"We're all good here," replies Carrie. "Hey, are you still painting pictures? I know Blake was always telling us that you're so good at your hobby. He said you never made any money, but it was a good hobby and kept you busy."

Tali bristles at the words and the insinuations. She carefully words her response. "I'm not sure what to make of that, Carrie."

She feels Blake, through Sam, is using Carrie to get information about her, but why? She later makes a note to on her cell phone to bring this up with her therapist, Shannon.

60

Putting the Puzzle Pieces Together

At her next appointment with Shannon, the pieces of this giant jigsaw puzzle of her life begin to connect. Shannon first asks, "Have you ever heard the term 'flying monkey'?"

Tali vaguely remembers Shannon using the term before but asks for a refresher. Shannon explains that it is a term related to a famous classic movie that had scenes featuring fictitious monkeys that could fly. They did the bidding of their wicked master. Shannon warns Tali, "In your case, Blake could be priming the pump by indicating to others, including Carrie, that he can't figure out whether what you say is true or false. That way later on, when you reach a point when you share more widely what you were experiencing, it will come across as a lie, and people you both know will trust him more than you. These could include not only friends but also family. Be aware that Blake, at some point, may put on the mask of being your victim rather than the reverse. And he is likely to be very believable to others. And , it's time to talk about the co-dependency aspect of narcissistic victimized relationships. While the victim continues to give of themselves and their empathetic caring gifts of trying to help the narcissist heal from their emotional neglectful upbringing... the narcissist continues to take life and love from the victim... the co-dependency equation stems from each factor... independent and dependent... needing to feel needed by the other person... sad but so true in today's world.

Dear Josie... I'm learning so much about Blake's personality disorder. Shannon is teaching me about narcissistic personalities. And I'm rereading the book Shannon recommended, Stop Walking on Eggshells. *I'm also doing some research on my own. Main message: I am not alone. This personality disorder is prevalent throughout society, but not many people are willing to speak up and state that they are victims of narcissists. It's time to speak up! I'm willing and able to do that. Right now. Blake's upbringing and family dynamics with his narcissistic mother have apparently had a lifetime effect on his life. Victims of narcissists need outside help. A message that needs to be shared: A victim cannot look too happy or too sad... Be wary of providing the narcissist with needed ammunition. The victims of emotional, mental, and physical abuse by narcissists need to get together and have a voice. Let's show up and point out for ourselves and our families how narcissistic partners are hurting and devastating lives. I'm done with this fake relationship and his fake love. He's only trying to control me.*

61

Garage Meltdown...
Do You Trust Me?

't's been a long day. No, it's been a long week,' Tali thinks as she pulls her car into the garage at seven o'clock on a Friday evening. Blake is in Las Vegas on a business trip, or he says it's a business trip. Tali turns off the engine and sits in the quiet for a moment. Her mind is racing. Work has been hard. She can't seem to focus on the new project. She's tired. Tears form in her eyes as she starts to cry. At first, she looks upward to keep the tears from rolling down her face and tells herself, 'Don't cry. Don't cry. Don't cry.' But she can't stop. Through the tears, she says out loud, "I can't do this anymore. I don't know what to do."

She cries out, "I can't keep going on like this...sad...depressed...unhappy. What is happening to me? Why is Blake so passive-aggressive toward me? One minute, he hates me, the next minute, he's offering to make coffee for me. Seriously? He always says I'm the one to blame for our problems. That just can't be true. I need help. I can't handle Blake's behaviors anymore." She continues to cry.

In that moment, a thought crosses her mind, a question: "Do you trust me?"

She stops crying and ponders the question. "Do I trust myself? No. Do I trust Blake? No." She feels an embracing and calming presence wash over her. Could this be a moment like what she and her Mamita were talking about while they were at the beach a few weeks ago? Maybe God is trying to reach out to her. She closes her tear-filled eyes, sinking into the silence. She is shaking and doesn't realize she's been sitting in the car crying for thirty minutes. She feels drained—emotionally, mentally, and physically. She continues to sit there thinking about the question. She decides to answer, "Yes, God, I trust you."

After a few more quiet minutes in the car, she opens the car door, grabs her computer bag out of the back seat, and enters the townhouse. Jasper is wagging her tail and jumping up and down with excitement that Mommy is home! Tali sits down with Jasper and pets and hugs this beautiful dog who truly loves her unconditionally. Misty senses that Tali is upset, as felines do, and wanders over to purr quietly and rub against Tali's leg. After a few minutes, Tali jumps up to grab Jasper's leash to go for a short walk before dinner. They loop around the complex. When they return home, Tali gets Jasper's dinner and fills her water bowl. She tells Jasper that they will go for a longer walk after dinner. Jasper excitedly eats her dinner. Tali inspects the contents of the fridge. She's not really hungry. She grabs a sparkling water and takes it out onto the terrace. While watching the afterglow of the sunset, Tali exclaims out loud once again, "I can't do this anymore! I'm not strong enough. I'm not enough. I just can't do this." She sobs uncontrollably.

Once again, she feels God asking, "Do you trust Me? I have brought you this far. I am not going to leave you now." Tali sits in silence while tears fall into her lap.

62

Is There a Cure?

Tali returns to Shannon's office the next Thursday afternoon promptly at two o'clock and settles into the recliner as Shannon enters and sits down at her desk. She notices Tali's eager expression and says, "You look like you have a question."

Tali responds, "Shannon, is there any cure for narcissism?"

Shannon looks Tali straight in the eye. "You're jumping ahead. But I'll stop where we were and respond. Unfortunately, there's likely not a cure. Current psychological research supports this. The major drawback is since a narcissist believes he is always right, he needs no help from anyone. It is his likely opinion that everyone around him has the problems. There is no standard counseling, no medications, no brain surgery that can fix this. The only glimpse of hope is if he does start psychotherapy and sticks with it, it may help bring about an attitude shift and an understanding of how his difficult behavior can hurt the people in his life. But it cannot create a new heart that has un-conditional love."

Tali starts sobbing uncontrollably. Finally, after about fifteen minutes, Shannon says, "Tali, let's call it a day for now and re-group next week to pick up the pieces. I'll share some tools and options you can use to try to somewhat mitigate the hell you are living in. I know you and I have not talked about faith as it relates to religion, but I want you to know I have been and will be praying for you."

Tali silently leaves the office and wanders to her car. Once she gets in and locks the door, she screams a primal, guttural sound and begs God to fix this. Shaking, she calls Molly, need-ing to settle down, too upset to drive.

Luckily, Molly answers on the third ring. "Hi, Tali. How's it going, girl?" Then she hears Tali's loud, large sobs and some-thing to the effect that "Shannon just told me that Blake is a narcissist and he will never get better."

"Where are you? Can I meet you somewhere right now? I can leave work a bit early today. No problem."

Molly drives to Shannon's office to pick up Tali and take her to dinner. She listens as Tali unloads her thoughts and fears about Blake and their marriage.

63

F.E.A.R. of the Unknown

Later that evening while sitting at her desk, Tali looks out her office window as the sun is setting on yet another day. She is trying to focus on the design project she got assigned two months ago. Blake's behaviors and outbursts are worsening in frequency and duration. She still can't understand why he acts the way he does. She wonders what is going to happen to her and starts talking out loud. "Will I ever be happy again? Will Blake and I ever be in love like we used to be? Or were we ever really in love?" She starts crying.

Sydney hears Tali's quiet sobs as she's passing by and pokes her head into Tali's semi-darkened office. "Tali?"

Tali continues to cry and doesn't respond. Sydney knocks as she enters the room. "Tali, want to talk?" Tali says between sobs, "Don't feel like talking." Sydney leaves her alone.

64

F.E.A.R. of Another Person

Tali walks down to the beach from the townhouse one evening before dinner. Blake called earlier to tell her he has a work dinner tonight, so he would call her later. As she wanders along the shore, she thinks about the recent conversations with Blake and his increasingly frequent rages at her. Why would one human being want to create fear in another human being? To make one person live in fear of them? Tali is trying to understand why Blake wants to hurt her and cause everyone who knows her and respects her to doubt her sanity. Why?

Her walk allows her time to think. The sound of the ocean waves always calms her and helps her realize that God is so much bigger than anything that is going on in her life. She returns to the townhome. Jasper and Misty greet her at the door. She is thankful Blake won't be calling right away. She needs some time to research something Shannon brought up at their last session, F.E.A.R.: *face everything and rise* or *fear everything and run*. As she feeds Jasper and Misty, she recognizes that these two loving pets are not fearful; they have love and food and a safe place to live. She wonders, 'Why am I so fearful these days? I'm fearful of Blake and what he might do to me, what he has already done to me. I didn't used to be afraid. I used to be happy and confident and very optimistic. What's happening to me?'

She makes a small salad as she's not very hungry. She picks up her iPad and takes it and her dinner outside to the terrace table. As she sips her sparkling water and picks at her salad, she scrolls through the search results on the concept of fear. Basically, she learns that fear is not tangible. It's a belief that something or someone could cause you harm. Individuals feel threatened when they feel fear on any of three planes: rational, primal, and irrational. 'Interesting,' she thinks. 'I have been allowing Blake to cause me to be fearful. I've let him steal my joy. I'm starting to understand what's happening to me. I still have a ways to go to stop further damage and work on undoing the damage he's already done to me and my family and friends. I can't wait to meet with Shannon tomorrow!'

65

The Playbook

Tali shows up ten minutes early for her now-standing one-hour appointment each Thursday to meet with Shannon. She looks forward to this hour as Shannon works with her on her relationship with Blake. Last week, Shannon indicated that Blake was a narcissist, a term she's added to the dictionary of her life. Tali is curious to see how Shannon will direct their session today.

Tali feels as though she is following a yellow brick road behind Amy to Shannon's office. Amy ushers her into the room, saying, "Shannon is running a bit behind as she wraps up a meeting with a couple in the conference room, but she'll be here in no more than five minutes." Amy then closes the door. Tali spots the recliner that she claims as her seat and slides into it. To her, it reminds her of her maternal grandfather's chair that was in their living room. She recalls that it was a special place to her throughout her childhood whenever her family visited. 'So is this chair today,' she thinks.

She recognizes the sound of Shannon's footsteps approaching. The door opens. In one smooth motion, Shannon grabs Tali's file plus legal pad and pen while pulling the side chair into place.

"Good afternoon, Tali. How was your week?" she inquires, sounding a bit scripted, but Tali attributes it to the fact that she is not Shannon's only client.

"Blake was up and down emotionally, including one intense rage at me," replied Tali. "But in the midst of it, I silently reminded myself of what you said earlier. That he is not allowed to flip my Glad and Gloomy switches. That alone helped me get through it. It did seem to upset him when he couldn't get the emotions he was looking for out of me."

"Great job, Tali. That is a really super step in setting boundaries. We will be building you an anti-narcissist toolbox that will help you. Let's get going. As you probably recall, I shared with you that my initial assessment is that Blake is more than likely what we psychology professionals refer to as a narcissist. Please be aware that I am using this term very broadly as there is a wide spectrum of personality issues that this term can cover. To gently test your recall, can you remember about a half dozen key symptoms that indicate that Blake is a narcissist?"

Tali replied with her brows furrowed, "I think I can. First, I remember the Greek guy who couldn't stop looking at his reflection in the pool of water. I know Blake takes a lot of selfies and posts them on Facebook. Maybe that's why they call them selfies because it stands for selfishness. I remember you indicated that a narcissist only cares about himself and does not have feelings for others. I picked up on that in Blake this past week. It was evident in the way he not only acted toward me, but also in the way he acted toward my friends."

"Good recall, Tali," commented Shannon. "Being selfish and not having empathy for others are absolutely two of the main signs of narcissism. Remember that we are all God's creatures and all sin to a degree in these areas of our lives. But what we are talking about in the case of individuals wired like Blake is very, very extreme. Continue."

"You talked about a person like this feeling extremely insecure inside. And that the person wears a mask to try to hide his insecurity to try to fool everybody until he runs out of some kind of strange, creepy power."

"Yes, the mask and the power supply," confirmed Shannon. "Tell me more."

Tali continues, "A narcissist evidently must have something called a power supply from somebody else. Like Blake seems to have to be in control all the time to have power over us. He makes me or my friends unhappy when we are having a good time in order to recharge his power like a battery. He can also be jealous of our happiness, including when we are happy being around other people."

"Excellent. That is at least a half dozen signs," Shannon said in a reassuring tone. "You're obviously an excellent listener with strong recall. Those are great qualities to have to help you deal with Blake." Shannon goes on, "We're going to push forward now, so, listen closely. Tali, are you a sports fan, and if so, what is your favorite sport or sports?"

Tali responds, "Yes, I grew up in a sports family. I was a softball pitcher from grade school through college, and I was on an occasional church or company team after that. My two brothers who are older played baseball, basketball, football, and soccer. I love watching college and NFL football as well as Major League Baseball."

"Got it," said Shannon. "Tali, have you ever heard the term 'playbook'?"

"Yes," replies Tali. "It's like in football, a book that the coach and his staff have with the team's game plan. It has the specific plays."

"Perfect answer," says Shannon, nodding in agreement. "So, what I want to do is to help you build what I will refer to as a narcissist playbook based on Blake and the personality traits he exhibits related to narcissism. You mentioned in one of our earlier sessions that your life with Blake was very chaotic. What the playbook will do is form patterns out of his behavior and provide a game plan for you on how to deal with it to assist in diffusing its impact on you and, hopefully, on other people in Blake's life. Your homework for this week is to report back here next week with your observations of any behavior patterns that you see more clearly in Blake. That way, we can use this log to start working on specific reactions for you to deploy. It's sort of like sending in a play and executing it to defend yourself from Blake."

Shannon continues, "Since you were so good at recalling the generic key symptoms of narcissism, I'm jumping pretty quickly to this next step with you. But I'll be backtracking along the way and defining some terms typically associated with narcissism. Also, a new book on borderline personality disorder is about to come out by the authors of the first book I recommended. The title is *Stop Walking on Eggshells for Partners* by Paul T. Mason, MS and Randi Kreger. Okay? See you next week!"

Tali nods, gets up from the recliner, and goes out to her car, her head spinning with a replay of the session.

66

Seaside Cafe

At nine Monday morning, Tali's already at the office in her weekly work routine. Tali's Mamita texts her to let her know she's going to be in town on business and wants to have lunch the next day somewhere convenient to where Tali works. "Let's go to Seaside Cafe at 11:30 a.m. tomorrow. I'll get there early and get us a table. Try to stretch your lunch hour a bit, okay?' Tali quickly texts a thumbs-up.

The next day, Tali runs out of the office at 11:15 and trots a couple of blocks toward the café to meet her Mamita. She mutters to herself, "I need this quiet time with my Mamita… Blake has been so aggressive, so full of himself, so controlling…especially this morning. Simply getting myself out of the house has been an ordeal these past two days while Blake's been in town. Blake screaming that his socks were mismatched and that it was all my fault, even though months ago, he mandated that only he would do the laundry and has been. Yesterday, he called his big brother to complain about me and tell him what a loser he had married. Glad he's driving back to Monterey today."

Tali recalled running to the garage this morning and fastening her seat belt as she backed her car out as quickly and safely as she could. She could hear Blake ranting in the driveway and saw him in her rearview mirror. She wondered what the neighbors were thinking as she thought, 'Why is Blake so mad at me? Why does he have to be so mean? He's supposed to drive back to his job in Monterey today.'

As Tali attempts to walk calmly into the restaurant, she spots her Mamita holding a table in the far corner.

"Well, hello!" Mamita gives her a big squeezing hug, noticing that Tali has lost weight she really didn't need to lose. She notices that her two shoes are alike but not the same color and that she wears no makeup nor jewelry. The highlights in her hair are overdue. This is not the Tali she has always known. She senses something major is wrong. Tali always looks at life with the glass half full, not half empty. She never wants to share anything negative. Mamita thinks she will have to very gently, but efficiently, try to get some updates out of her over lunch.

Trying to be upbeat, Tali responds, "Great to see you and catch up!"

Mamita says, "I went ahead and ordered your usual Cobb salad with two servings of ranch dressing on the side and water to drink. I'm having low-carb veggies and a house side salad with water. I'm trying to shed a few pounds before heading to the Florida beaches with some friends in a couple of weeks."

Tali nods and speaks softly, "How is everyone back home? Miss seeing them. I think I need to come home to visit. Let's get everyone together before the last month of summer flies by.

That would be grand to try and do. We could hang out at the beach and play volleyball. I need some downtime. I'm trying to schedule our trip to Miami to see Danielle in August. Danielle purchased a new sailboat that she wants to show me. I haven't seen her in two years. Will be nice to catch up." She doesn't know in her heart if she really wants to go on a vacation given Blake's behavior this morning and, quite frankly, given his behavior most every day over the past several months.

Tali and her Mamita chat about this and that as Tali picks at her salad and her mother scarfs hers down. She notices that her Mamita is staring at her hair, her eyes, and her earlobes repetitively. Tali finally says in her little daughter voice, "I know you're staring at my disheveled look today and wondering what is wrong."

Mamita responds, "You better believe I am. So, what's wrong, my dear?"

Tali's eyes immediately fill with tears. "I'm sorry, Mamita. I can't get into it right now, since I need to run back to work. But…it's Blake."

"Okay, but let's talk about this another time. I'm worried about you."

67

More Terminology

Tali shows up on Thursday for another one-hour session with Shannon. Teaming up with Shannon to learn more terminology and develop her personal playbook has been on her mind big time.

"Okay, Tali, how was your week?" Shannon asks.

"Blake was all over the place emotionally, including one morning when he stood in the driveway yelling at me as I drove away to go to work," Tali summarizes, anxious to get into today's agenda. "He's in Monterey now, but he's coming back almost every weekend, which is so uncomfortable. I need as many tools as I can gather."

Shannon replies, "Be aware that going forward, as you implement the tools I share with you to help you manage Blake, that it may cause his power level to go down as he gets less of it directly from you…which is one reason he comes back on the weekend. He may very well rage at you, and possibly your family and friends, using them as an additional power source. We'll need to focus on how to deal with that as well. If at any time he becomes physically violent with you or with any loved ones, you should call 911. It will most likely result in a police report, but you really have no choice. From what you've shared, it doesn't appear likely to happen, but you never know. I want you to be prepared for whatever is around the corner as much as possible."

Tali shares "the fall" story/mystery that she never truly got the answers for what actually happened that night, especially after her very lucid dream about Blake hitting her and her falling against the bathroom towel rack.

Shannon takes notes and says, "Tali, that is cause for alarm. Be on guard." She continues, "Your homework assignment for this week was to report back today with your observations of any behavior patterns that you can now see more clearly in Blake. Recall that this will allow us to start working on specific reactions for you to deploy, like selecting a play from the playbook to help you defend yourself from Blake. Note that for now, we're concentrating on playing defense, but we want to have a goal of you playing primarily offense so that you are staying ahead of Blake by having a good idea of which play he's going to try to run in advance."

Tali volunteers, "When he works here on the weekends, I've noticed some a pattern, like when he gets home, he always does the same routine, ending with a beer in a koozie. I never know which Blake will walk through the door, never know which way the wind is blowing, how his day has been, who he blames for negative stuff happening during his day. I wish I had a Blake barometer app to alert me to what's going to be his mood when he enters our home. He's usually in a bad mood. He grabs a beer, then ends up cutting me down and yelling at me. Then he falls asleep on the sofa. The next morning, he starts yelling at me because I didn't wake him up and let him sleep on the sofa. If I do wake him up and he comes to bed, then he makes me have sex with him. He makes me do it every day we're together. Even after the car wreck, before I could even walk again, he made me." Tali begins to cry. She says through her tears, "I'm just not into the everyday thing. There's more to love and marriage than that. At least, that's what all my friends tell me."

Shannon remarks, "Perfect, but a very painful example. Let's pick up where we left off last week by going through key terminology and phrases used to build what I earlier referred to as a playbook based on Blake and his narcissistic tendencies, including typical manipulations, such as gaslighting." Shannon pauses and tells Tali to watch an old movie called *Gaslight* released in 1944. "He will try to use your friends and family — the 'flying monkeys' — to gaslight you; 'hoovering' to try to get you back; and love bombing with attention, trips, and gifts. I also want you to learn how to be a 'grey rock,' which means talking a lot without saying anything that can be used to hurt you by Blake or the people he's trying to turn against you."

After they finish the session, Tali goes out to her car. She feels like her life right now is like a jigsaw puzzle with many pieces missing.

68

Awakening...

Early one Saturday morning about five, Tali wakes up and tiptoes as if walking on eggshells to the kitchen. Blake is uncharacteristically still asleep, as are Jasper and Misty.

She makes herself a single-serve K-Cup of a strong French roast coffee, adding a splash of her favorite vanilla-flavored creamer. She grabs her Bible and her daily yearlong devotional. She always hides them in an unfilled corner inside an old buffet in the dining room, a family hand-me-down. Having her Bible and other religious books out in broad daylight in the house seems to upset Blake, so she has resorted to this hideaway, apologizing to God occasionally in a silent prayer. She quietly opens the French doors and creeps out to the terrace. She immediately feels the slightly cool summer breeze. She sits down in a wooden rocking chair in a corner of the terrace that was formed by the exterior brick of the fireplace in the hearth room. The potted plants appear thirsty for a drink of water from the previous 90-degree day.

She says an "ACTS" prayer to God, whispering first her worshipful Adoration of God, followed by Confession of her sins, then next giving Thanksgiving for God's Son Jesus who died for everyone's sins with the promise of forgiveness, and lastly Supplication, where she asks God to meet not only her needs, but the needs of others. She always concludes by praying for things like strength, wisdom, guidance, comfort, and safety for herself and her family and friends, as well as protection from the mental stresses that she experiences daily. And, yes, she concludes with a prayer for Blake, asking God for help in forgiving him for what he has done to her, is doing to her, and will do to her. She could not go to that place of forgiveness without Him.

Tali has been going to counseling weekly with Shannon for a while now and it has opened her eyes. The narcissistic relationship has ironically shoved her into an awakening spiritually. Blake and his narcissism have nearly destroyed her faith in him and absolutely undermined her confidence and ability to trust anyone. Sometimes she struggles to string two sentences together containing a common thread. Some days, she can't even complete two sentences. She feels as if it has almost destroyed her, throwing her into a depression where she questions life itself.

But this morning, she glimpses thoughts she's never had before. Like no matter how horrific this ordeal is, this walk through fire is becoming spiritually freeing. It has erased the major fears in her life. And if fear dares to try to return, she knows how to ask the Great Counselor to free it from keeping her in bondage. This is so tough to endure, but this has been a wake-up call for her relationship with God.

After an hour spent in prayer and devotion, Tali strides back into the house, letting the screen and glass doors make their normal sounds as she firmly opens and closes them. Her feet make the wooden floors in the hearth room creak. She places her Bible and devotional book on the coffee table in the family room. She then goes into the kitchen to make her second cup of coffee, complete with sound effects, as if Blake were not even in the house.

She feels free. She feels renewed. She feels peace that surpasses all understanding.

69

The Last Straw

"Hey," Blake says as he enters the family room on Sunday afternoon. Tali sits in the wing-backed chair with her sketch pad on her lap. With the end of her art pencil in the corner of her mouth, she glances up at him and says, "Hey."

He sits down in his usual spot on the sofa and says, "Tali, we need to talk. I have to go to New York for a few days on business. Will you be okay here without me?"

Surprise registering on her face, Tali replies, "Of course I'll be fine here. Why do you ask?"

"You've been a little distant lately. I'm concerned about you," he says.

She replies, "Don't worry about me. I've got a lot on my mind right now. That's all."

"Anything you wanna talk about?"

"No. Not now," she says as she studies her drawing and touches up some shadowing while she talks. "When do you leave?"

He replies, "Tomorrow afternoon, and I'll be back on Thursday."

"Okay," she says. She goes back to studying her drawing and touching up a few lines here and there.

Blake gets up from the sofa and grabs his laptop off the coffee table. He leaves the room to go pack his suitcase for tomorrow's flight. About an hour later, he returns to the family room. Tali is still sitting there with her sketch pad. He says, "What should we do for dinner?"

She answers, "There are two steaks in the fridge. How about we grill them tonight since you'll be gone this week? I'll make a Caesar salad and roast some corn. Sound good?"

"Yes," he replies enthusiastically. "I'll go season the meat."

Tali sits there quietly for a few more minutes. Then, she closes her sketch pad and climbs the stairs to her art room. The door has been closed. She opens the door and, as she enters the room, notices that her notes and brushes are not where she left them yesterday. It appears certain items have been moved aside like someone was looking for something. She knows Jasper and Misty have not been in here and wonders if Blake could have been looking for a pencil or something in here. 'So odd,' she thinks. 'It doesn't look like anything is missing, just moved.'

Talking softly to herself, she says, "He knows this is my space and that my notes and files are kept in a particular order based on ideas for work projects, some ideas for personal projects, and some ideas for the patients at the rehabilitation hospital. I'll ask him later." She places her sketch pad on the drafting table and then closes the door behind her as she exits the room, going downstairs to the kitchen. She asks Blake, "Were you looking for something in my art room? My files and brushes aren't in the same places I left them yesterday."

Blake looks up from his task of seasoning the steaks with a blank stare on his face. "No, baby, you must be imagining things. You probably put things in different places because you were in a hurry to get ready to go see the movie yesterday, remember?" Blake hopes she buys his reasoning. He thought he had put everything back correctly while he was snooping in Tali's art room last night. He was looking for some of her work files so that he could contact her clients and convince them that she's not fit. Eventually, he thinks, Sydney will become weary of all the clients complaining about Tali and fire her. Then she would have to come to Monterey to live with him. He took photos of the work files he found. He's planning to study these clients while on his flight to NYC.

"Oh, yeah, okay." Tali plays along with him then heads back upstairs to her art room to investigate. As she looks through her work project files, she notices that the design pages and itemized invoices aren't in the correct order for her filing system. And she always files each project in alphabetical order by client name. "Since when does N come before L?" she asks, knowing Blake has been rooting through her files. But why? She texts Sydney to schedule a meeting the next morning. She closes the door as she leaves the room to go back downstairs to the kitchen to prep the salad and corn, all the time wondering what Blake is up to and why it's making her so nervous.

The following morning, Blake finishes packing for his trip. He kisses her goodbye before she leaves the townhouse. They each drive away with some pretty intense thoughts running through their minds. Blake is planning his review of Tali's clients and his interaction with Bentley in NYC. Tali is wondering why Blake was snooping through her project files. What was he searching for? She can't wait to talk with Sydney this morning.

Tali climbs the stairs to her office and tosses her keys and briefcase on the chaise before she heads over to Sydney's office. She knocks and Sydney motions her in while she wraps up a phone call. "Hey, dear," Sydney says. "What's up?"

Tali comes in and sits down in a chair facing her. "I don't know what's going on. Blake has been snooping in my art room. My files are out of order, especially my work project files. It appears he's looking for something, but what, I'm not sure."

"That's a bit alarming, Tali," Sydney says. "Which work files were out of order?"

Tali responds, "Let me think. Newport Beach Convention Center, Landmark Offices, Hunter Polo Club, and Master's Golf Shop. All kind of in the middle of the alphabet."

Sydney says, "Just for due diligence, let's reach out to each of your clients either today or tomorrow to touch base. You get my drift?"

"Yes, ma'am. I get it," Tali says. "Do you really think Blake might try to sabotage me with my clients?"

"I don't know, but I wouldn't put anything past him," Sydney replies. Tali nods and returns to her own office, stopping by Beth's desk to request tangible files on all of her current clients be brought to her office by this afternoon.

Meanwhile, Blake drives to the airport. He's planning to sit in the airport lounge and review the photos he took of Tali's work files while he waits for his plane to board. And he has a Zoom call with his office in Monterey at noon. He told Tali that his trip to NYC is for business, but he told his boss and administrative assistant that he's taking personal days this week. He's waiting to contact Bentley when he arrives in NYC so as not to arouse suspicion in Bentley's mind and reduce the chances of Bentley calling Tali to tell her he's visiting Bentley. Blake orders coffee and opens the photos app on his phone. He pulls a notebook and pen out of his backpack to begin taking notes on what he's seeing.

****

It's evening in New York when the plane lands. Blake exits, smiling at the flight attendant. His phone buzzes. It's Tali. She's asking if his flight was good. He quickly types, "Good flight. About to grab taxi and head to hotel. Xoxo" He walks past baggage claim and outside to the taxi stand. After hailing a taxi, he climbs into the back seat and gives the driver the hotel name. He's staying at a hotel in the financial district where Bentley works. Upon arriving at the hotel, the porter takes his bag and backpack up to his room. He tips the porter sparingly. Blake stretches out on the king-sized bed and stares at his phone. He pulls up Bentley's contact info and texts him: "Hey! I'm in town for a few days. Let's meet up for drinks and dinner. How about tomorrow?"

A minute later, his phone buzzes. Bentley replies, "Sure. How about Manny's Bar and Grill on 15th at 7:00 p.m. tomorrow?" Blake replies, "Sounds good! CU then." He rolls over and closes his eyes while he plans his conversation with Bentley.

Bentley calls Tali.

Tali answers, "Hey, what's up?"

"I just received a text from Blake. He's here in NYC and wants to meet up for drinks and dinner tomorrow. I agreed. What is he doing here?"

Tali says, "I don't exactly know. He's been snooping around my art room and going through my work project files. I'm concerned. He told me that he's on a business trip there, but I kind of doubt that. He always says his boss doesn't like him and never puts him in front of clients since he screwed up that meeting with the multibillion-dollar CEO a few months ago. I think I'll call his administrative assistant to get the name of his hotel in NYC. She would have been the one to book his hotel if it's truly a business trip. I'll let you know what I find out before you hang out with him. When are you two getting together?"

"Tomorrow night at seven o'clock."

"Okay," says Tali. "I'll text you when I learn something."

"Sounds cool. Thanks, Turt. *Ciao.*"

"*Ciao,*" says Tali, and they both end the call. Tali sits down at her drafting table to go over a design she was working on Friday. Thinking about the ideas she had for improvement yesterday while she was drawing, she begins lightly sketching.

A couple hours later, Beth knocks on Tali's office door and enters carrying a stack of client files. Tali's on the phone and motions her to place the files on her desk. She holds up her index finger to ask her to wait a minute. She finishes the phone call and says, "Thanks, Beth. I'll try to keep the files in order for you. I know you have an amazing filing system!"

They laugh, and Beth says, "Thanks, Tali. Is there anything I can help you with? Reviewing the files for what purpose?"

Tali crosses behind her and closes the door. She says, "Blake's been snooping through my work files in my art room at home. For what reason, I don't know. Sydney and I decided that I should reach out to each of my clients to touch base today or tomorrow while Blake's out of town. Sydney has a feeling that he's up to something, and you know Sydney's intuition is always spot-on!"

Beth agrees, "Yeah, true. I can help you make calls when you're ready. Just let me know."

"Thanks! We'll probably start tomorrow morning. I'll be reviewing each client file this afternoon. Thanks for bringing the files to me."

"You're welcome, Tali. Give me the green light and which calls you want me to make, and I'll get on it. Catch you later." Beth leaves as Tali grabs a few files and settles into the chaise. She begins to take notes on each file.

Blake's lying on the bed with his phone beside his head. When it buzzes, he realizes that he had dozed off. He stands up, stretches, and goes to the bathroom to freshen up. He grabs a polo shirt and a blue blazer out of his suit bag. A few minutes later, he leaves his room and heads to the elevator, thinking, 'I'm in NYC for a few days, might as well see the sights.' Outside, he heads toward a row of bright neon signs with the sounds of live bands permeating the lulls between the screeching tires and honking horns of traffic. He walks a little further and the background noise fades. He hears a combo playing one of his favorite songs and stops to check out the menu board beside the front entrance. 'Looks good,' he thinks and enters. He sits at the bar while he waits for a table to become available. When seated, he peruses the menu and orders. He leans back in his chair and listens to the band while he nurses a beer. He spends the evening alone while thinking through his plan for this trip.

When Tali comes into the townhouse, Jasper jumps up to greet her and Misty purrs from her perch across the room. Tali plays with them for a few minutes and then fills their water bowls. She grabs Jasper's leash and leads Jasper out the door for a stroll to the beach. They walk along the shore for a while before Tali stops to breathe deeply and stare out at the waves. So many thoughts run through her mind. She's tired of Blake's lies. She caught him in another one today. When she called his admin in Monterey, she told Tali that Blake was taking personal days this week and she has no knowledge of which hotel he is staying at in NYC. His admin didn't even know that Blake flew to NYC.

'Wow…' Tali thinks. 'I can't go on like this. I'll probably learn more about his antics after his dinner with Bentley and my calls to clients tomorrow." She stands there as the ebbing tide washes the sand away around her toes. She stands there as long as she can, thinking about the sand washing away around her, just like her young marriage was washing away.

The next morning, Tali climbs the stairs to her office floor. She stops to talk with Beth, and they decide to meet up in an hour to start calling the list of clients, sharing updates and just checking in. She's eager to talk with Bentley tonight after his dinner with Blake. In her office, she checks email and reviews her calendar for the day. Beth comes in an hour later, and they divide up the stack of client files to start calling. After about three hours, Beth comes back to Tali's office with her stack of files. "All calls went well. They're aware to not take any calls or messages from Blake. Your clients absolutely love you, Tali! They all said to tell you that they're thinking about you. How did your call list go?"

"Good," says Tali a bit pensively. She continues, "They're all pleased with our work so far. But one client says someone impersonating a potential client contacted him this morning before

I called. He said this person heard that I was designing some retail space for them and wanted to know my client's opinion of me. He said he was shopping for an interior designer. Then he told my client that he had heard some rumors about me. I reassured the client that Blake's call was bogus, and I apologized for Blake's behavior. I think I smoothed everything over, but I'm putting this client's project at the top of my list to finish the project ahead of schedule. No reason to test their loyalty at this point."

Beth sighs. She feels sorry for Tali having to go through this situation with Blake. She gives Tali a hug then leaves her office.

Tali stares out the window for a few minutes and then picks up her red journal and nestles into the chaise. Although it's lunchtime, she's not hungry. She decides to write.

Dear Josie… I'm so confused. Blake told me that he was going to NYC on business, but his office says he's taking personal days this week. And he called one of my clients trying to place doubts in my client's mind about me. And he's having drinks and dinner with Bentley tonight! What's he up to? He won't give me a straight answer about anything these days. I don't know what to believe anymore. Shannon and I were talking about gaslighting and manipulation last week. She says that narcissists and controlling people use gaslighting techniques to cause people in their lives to doubt their reality. I can relate to that! Blake's constant yelling and raging at me, claiming that every bad thing that happens is my fault, even if I wasn't even present. Telling me that I'm crazy and never right… seriously? What is he trying to do to me? He makes rude comments to me and then gets mad at me when I get upset about what he said. I look forward to meeting with Shannon this week. And I think it's time…time to call Molly's attorney, Jay Richards. I need to have a plan of action. I'll call Jay tomorrow.

At 9:30 p.m., Tali is sitting in her art room with Jasper and Misty looking over a design that she's presenting to Sydney the next morning. Her phone rings. It's Bentley. "Hey!" she says. "How was your evening with Blake?"

"Just let me tell you girl… OMG…your hubby is a piece of work, and that's putting it nicely. He spent the entire evening talking about himself and how great he is at his job and how he wants to guide me through building my business when Tesca and I move back to California in a few years. He went on and on and on. How do you do it? I mean, listen to his verbal rubbish day in and day out? I'm sorry if I'm being kinda rude right now, but I've been through something tonight just listening to him for two hours. Then he started in on you and your sanity."

"What?!" exclaims Tali. "My sanity? What did he say?"

"He says you've been acting distant and absent-minded lately. He says your self-esteem is low, and you're doubting your purpose in life."

"That's bullshit!" says Tali. "I'm fine! Better than ever, actually! He's the one who's ticking off everyone he comes in contact with, including his boss and coworkers. He told me this trip was business, but his admin says he told them he was taking personal days this week. What's he up to?"

"I don't know, Turt, but I think you need to get out of there. I think Blake's about to snap, and I don't want you anywhere near him. I'm coming to Newport Beach before Blake returns to be there in case he starts anything. What day is he supposed to return?"

"Thursday," she says.

"Okay, then. I'll arrive Wednesday afternoon, and we can have dinner and hang out. I'm here for you. I got your back."

"Thanks, dude. You're the best."

"Hey, we've been through a lot all these years. You've always had my back, girl. Now it's my turn. See you tomorrow."

Tali puts down her phone and ponders the whole conversation. She lays down on the chaise with Jasper by her side and Misty on top of a throw pillow. Both pets are sound asleep. Tali pulls a blanket up around her chin and settles there to not wake the pets. She reaches for her phone to set an alarm for the morning and then extinguishes the light.

Morning light shines through the eastern windows as her alarm beeps. Jasper and Misty stretch and yawn and snuggle closer to Tali. She turns off the alarm and lays there for a moment of calm before she has to face the day. Then she gets up and goes downstairs with two sleepy pets right behind her. She turns on the coffee pot and grabs a cold water out of the fridge on her way to pick up Jasper's leash. She and Jasper go outside to begin their morning walk to the beach. The sky is glowing, and Tali tells herself that this will be a beautiful day, even with everything swirling around her. After her meeting with Sydney to review her proposed design, she'll call Jay Richards, the attorney whom Molly recommended. Then she has a new client call at two and a follow-up call with the client that Blake attempted to instigate a schmear campaign on her. She thinks she can finish their project early next week, below budget and ahead of schedule. Then she'll go home to take care of the pets before meeting Bentley for dinner. He'll be staying at a nearby hotel. Even though they've been friends forever, they decided it would be best for Bentley not to be staying at the townhouse when Blake returns tomorrow. Although he'll be close enough to come over if Blake rages and Tali needs him.

'How did all this happen?' She thinks about the whole situation while she and Jasper head back to the townhouse. 'Well, at least there's a plan.'

At noon, Bentley texts Tali to say that he's on his way and his plane will land at 6:00 p.m. She texts back and throws out a few restaurant ideas. They decide on a place. Each texts, "*Ciao.*"

Tali scrolls through the contact list on her phone. "Here's the number Molly gave me for her attorney, Jay Richards," she says out loud. She places the call.

"Jay Richards," a person answers.

Tali says, "Hi, Mr. Richards. I'm Tali Solace, and my friend Molly Anderson recommended you."

"Oh, yes, Molly. She's a firecracker and so smart! How's she doing these days?"

"She's doing very well. She speaks so highly of you."

Jay says, "Thank you for sharing the compliment. What can I do for you, Tali?"

"I think I need to leave my husband. We've been married for four years and now he's trying to sabotage my career and ruin my friendships. Not to mention his daily rages at me. He's currently on a trip to NYC, and he lied to me about it being a business trip. He's already contacted one of my best friends in New York and tried to slander me to my friend. Of course, my friend called me to tell me the details of what Blake is saying about me. I don't know what's going on with him, Mr. Richards." She sighs.

"Please call me Jay, Tali. And take a deep breath. That's a lot to deal with. I've been practicing law for over forty years. I've tried cases before that sound very similar to yours. Let's talk about this situation one piece at a time. So, you said you and… Blake, is it?…have been married for four years? Did you know him long before you were married?"

She replies, "Yes. We met in college, our junior year. We got married about a year after we graduated."

"Do you have any children?" he asks.

"No," she says. "Blake quit his job in Newport Beach and took another job in Monterey, so he's not always around. Which gives me a break from his rages and temper tantrums. Although he is quite adept at yelling at me over the phone and in text messages. He has sharpened those skills since he moved to Monterey."

"What is Blake's occupation?"

"Financial advisor."

"What is your occupation?"

She replies, "Interior designer."

"Who earns more money?"

"Our salaries are comparable at the moment."

"Okay," Jay continues, "How would you categorize your marriage right now? Salvageable? Irreconcilable? Broken? Irretrievable?"

Tali is silent as she thinks for a moment and then she says, "Broken and irreconcilable."

Jay says, "I'm so sorry you're going through this, Tali. I'll send you some forms to complete while you think about whether you want to file for divorce. If you decide to file, please send the completed forms back to me, and my associate will begin the filing process. Please feel free to call me with any questions.

I know this is new. Starting the divorce process can be scary. We're here for you if you decide that divorcing Blake is the solution to your problem. Take care, Tali. Please know that we will help you."

"Thank you, Mr. Richards…I mean Jay. Thank you so much. Bye for now."

"Bye, Tali. I'll send those forms to you right now."

They both end the call.

Epilogue

Tali goes to sleep knowing that phone call will completely alter the seemingly perfect life she's been living. She knows it's going to be painful. She also knows she feels broken and vulnerable. Just as it has taken time for her to recognize what is and isn't working in her relationship with Blake, she knows she will need time as an ally if she is to take control of her life. She doesn't know if she has the courage or the strength to make her next decisions and take action. Tali's family and friends will be there for her, but will their support be enough? Things are not what they seem to be.

Escaping Solace

Book Two of a Trilogy

The next book in this trilogy reveals how difficult it is to even *think* of separating from a life formed around (and by) an individual with a narcissistic personality disorder. It's dangerous. Tali knows it's dangerous, and once again, questions what happened when she woke up with blood on her face. Is she crazy? Is she being tormented and abused? Or is she overly emotional and sensitive? Join Tali in *Escaping Solace* and discover just how challenging it is for her to believe in herself when the person she loves the most, the person she was going to spend the rest of her life with, becomes a threat to everything and everyone she holds dear.

About the Author

Skye Bellarmine

Skye Bellarmine is an author who goes wherever the wind takes her. Her nomadic family was always moving, so she learned early to adapt to multiple environments and personality types. Skye's advanced studies have earned her a degree in life skills and her intuitive empathy has enabled her to learn from and rise above life's challenges. She doesn't take anything or anyone for granted and recognizes that the traumas in her life created her spirit, her spark, and her determination.

Breaking Solace is her first book. With the spirit of a brave warrior, her goal in writing is to help others gain the fortitude to stand up, stand out, and overcome abuse. Skye will help you ride the waves of life into a beautiful shore, teach you how to shine through the darkness and restart your life as many times as needed so that you can emerge as the gemstone you are meant to be.

https://starskyepress.com

email: skye@starskyepress.com